loaded

RECKLESS MC OPEY TEXAS CHAPTER

WALL STREET JOURNAL & USA TODAY BESTSELLING AUTHOR

KB WINTERS

Copyright and Disclaimer

This book is a work of fiction. The names, characters, places and incidents are products of the writer's imagination and have been used fictitiously and are not to be construed as real. Any resemblance to persons, living or dead, actual events, locales or organizations is entirely coincidental.

Copyright © 2019 Book Boyfriends Publishing

All rights reserved. No part of this publication may be reproduced, stored in or introduced into a retrieval system, or transmitted, in any form, or by any means (electronic, mechanical, photocopying, recording, or otherwise) without the prior written permission of the copyright owner. The author acknowledges the trademarked status and trademark owners of various products referenced in this work of fiction, which have been used without permission. The publication/use of the trademarks is not authorized, associated with, or sponsored by the trademark owners.

Table of Contents

Copyright and Disclaimer ii

Prologue 7

Chapter One 31

Chapter Two 39

Chapter Three 53

Chapter Four 59

Chapter Five 71

Chapter Six 87

Chapter Seven 101

Chapter Eight 109

Chapter Nine 117

Chapter Ten 133

Chapter Eleven 145

Chapter Twelve 157

Chapter Thirteen 165

Chapter Fourteen 179

Chapter Fifteen 187

Chapter Sixteen 205

Chapter Seventeen.. 215

Chapter Eighteen..227

Chapter Nineteen 237

Chapter Twenty 243

Chapter Twenty-One 257

Chapter Twenty-Two..269

Chapter Twenty-Three 279

Chapter Twenty-Four 293

Chapter Twenty-Five..303

Chapter Twenty-Six..325

Chapter Twenty-Seven 345

Chapter Twenty-Eight 353

Chapter Twenty-Nine.......................................365

LOADED

Reckless MC Opey Texas Chapter Book 4

By Wall Street Journal & USA Today Bestselling Author

KB Winters

Prologue

Annabelle ~ 3 months ago

There it was. The only barrier between me and a good time was the big red door that bore an uncanny resemblance to its namesake, a barn door. The door stood there, big, red, and imposing, goading me for being a damn coward. And I was because I was nervous as hell about going inside, knowing what waited on the other side.

The Barn Door was an exclusive, private sex club located on the ass end of Hardtail Ranch, but I wasn't sure how many people actually made the connection. The land was so vast and most people were trying to be discreet. Including me. As a respected and well known doctor in the small town of Opey, Texas, I had more than a few reasons to be nervous about stepping through that big red door. The last thing I wanted was a bunch of creepy cowboys stopping in the ER to get a glimpse of me during work hours. No thanks. Opey was a small town, and though most people respected each other's privacy, there was always at least one asshole in the bunch, and with my luck, he'd find me.

"The door ain't gonna bite ya."

The deep voice startled me. I turned with a gasp, getting ready to give this asshole a piece of my mind when the bluest eyes I'd ever seen came into view. Hell, those blue eyes were connected to the most handsome, gorgeous man I'd ever seen up close. None of that mattered, though, because it was all attached to the surliest asshole on the planet.

"Wheeler," I said, hoping my voice sounded strong and firm. "Hi." I stood there, staring at him while I tried to figure out if he was waiting for me to go inside or leave. Since there was no way to get out of this awkward encounter without making it more awkward, I shrugged as if I were leaving.

"Well, see you around," I said, which wasn't true. I never did see much of Wheeler, other than from a distance, like when I visited Peaches on the ranch. I turned in the direction of my car and walked away.

"Entrance is that way," his deep voice called out, full of amusement. At my expense, based on the laughter he didn't try to hide.

His words stopped my feet so fast I nearly walked right out of my sexy black stilettos.

"I changed my mind," I called to him over my shoulder. With my chin notched up high and my hands fisted on my hips, I turned and dared him to challenge me.

Which, of course, Wheeler was happy to do. "Don't do it on my account."

"I'm not," I insisted. There was no way in hell I'd ever let a man change my course in life. Again.

"Okay," he shot back, skepticism clear in his tone.

"I'm not."

This time he held up both hands in a defensive gesture, a smile splitting those lush pink lips into an enticing smile. Why did the good looking ones always have to be such jerks?

"Okay, I believe you Doc."

It would've been believable if his big blue eyes didn't show off the lie, proudly.

"Believe what you want." He would anyway, just like anyone else. "See you around, Wheeler."

"I'll walk you to your car," he said, already coming up to my side before I gave an answer.

"That's not necessary. I made it this far on my own, and I can make it back."

That was the mantra of the independent single woman, at least as far as I was concerned. The moment I got used to having someone around to help, they let me down when I needed them most.

"It ain't necessary, but maybe it'll make me feel better."

He flashed a gorgeous smile that I was sure would get him anything he wanted inside The Barn Door, which only made me wonder what in the hell he was doing out here with me.

Too bad for him I was only somewhat affected by that smile, gorgeous though it was. "Maybe going inside will make *you* feel better."

His lips twitched, but Wheeler said nothing, just stood a few feet away as I hit the button on the key fob to open the door. He watched me, an amused smile teasing the corners of his mouth, golden brown arms folded over his massive chest.

"Doubtful," he said, apparently aiming to master the one-word retort. He had more than amusement in his voice, but I couldn't recognize the emotion. The little I knew about Wheeler? He was an expert at hiding his emotions.

"Well, something other than standing here has to be part of your night."

"Eventually," he said. And waited.

Whatever. I slipped behind the steering wheel of my car and turned the key, but nothing happened. The car was just two years old so I wasn't worried, just pulled the key out and tried again. And again. And again.

"No," I silently pleaded. "Not now. Please don't do this to me, not right now."

A tap sounded on my window, and I didn't have to turn around to know it was Wheeler. But, of course, I did. That gorgeous face was so at odds with his bad attitude and that haunted quality he wore like a cloak that it kicked my heart rate up a notch. Or twenty.

"Problem?"

I groaned, "A couple," and pushed the door open, forcing him to step back.

To my surprise, he offered, "Maybe I can help."

I looked at him with suspicion. "Why would you do that?" He wasn't a bad guy as far as I could tell, but I didn't exactly have the greatest track record when it came to that kind of thing.

It was his turn to frown and look more than a little offended. "Why wouldn't I? I'm a nice guy."

A snort escaped my mouth, which was rude, considering he'd offered to help. "Yeah? You got any proof?" I just couldn't stop myself.

His lips kicked up into one of those casual, lazy grins that had my knees going wobbly, and I leaned against my car to avoid embarrassing myself.

"The proof is right here, with me taking a look at why your car won't start."

Before I could say anything, he had the hood up and handed me his phone with the flashlight app burning bright.

"Hold this," he ordered.

I glued my gaze to his forearms, golden brown from too many hours in the sun, with a thick coating of dark hair wrapped around them. They highlighted the muscles every time he moved. My mouth watered at the sight, which was when I realized I should've gone inside the barn, at least for my own sanity.

I had a reason for coming here, after months of avoiding the place. Plain and simple. Basic, no not basic, it was base. Put simply, I needed to get laid, and Wheeler was too tempting a choice.

And a terrible choice. A very terrible choice considering his connection to my only real friend in this whole damn town.

"So, what do you say?" Wheeler looked down at me, a smile playing on his lips and amusement dancing in his eyes.

I blinked, confused because I still had my gaze focused on his forearms and cooling the temperature of my body from said gaze. "About what?"

"Me. Giving you a ride home. You know, on account of your broken down car?"

"I thought you were going to fix it for me."

"Busted starter. We'll deal with getting it towed into town tomorrow. What'd you'd expect from a European tin can."

"European? And let me guess, Wheeler. You drive something big and American, probably a gas guzzler too." Because that would just make the stereotype complete, wouldn't it?

"If you say so, Doc." He always had to be so mysterious, didn't he?

Well, I wasn't intrigued by that particular mystery, so I waved a hand in front of us and sighed. "Then lead us to the paragon of American manufacturing brilliance and masculinity."

He gave me a look I couldn't decipher and began to walk. I followed behind, absolutely *not* staring at his long muscular legs. Or his ass that looked tight enough to bounce off a few quarters, a theory I was sorely tempted to test.

"Got me all figured out, huh, Doc?"

"Not at all." Some things I could figure out. He'd been in the military and come out with a pretty serious case of PTSD that he was doing his damnedest to hide from everyone. That didn't take a genius to diagnose, though. I'd seen enough cases of PTSD in emergency rooms throughout my career, from medical school in

Colorado and then completing my residency in Houston, a fellowship in Maryland and then moving to Opey. Gunshot wounds, domestic violence, random acts of crime, heart problems. It affected everyone differently. Too often, the effects stuck with them for a long time.

"Just a bit of deductive reasoning."

He snorted, and came to a stop beside a black monstrosity I could barely see in the darkness swamping the property.

"You like using big words, don't you?"

I blinked and let my gaze crawl up his body, stopping at his stupid handsome face.

"Oh, is this the part where you say something disparaging about 'smart chicks' or something equally unique?"

His blue gaze never left mine as his hands fisted on his hips, one dark brow lifted, challenging me. "See, all figured out."

LOADED

The man was so damn frustrating that a low growl came from somewhere deep inside my throat.

"Whatever, Wheeler." I rounded the big black SUV and waited for him to unlock the doors. Better to get this ride over as soon as possible.

***

"Thanks for the lift." Before Wheeler even had a chance to shift his car into park, I had the door open and one foot already on the newly paved driveway I had installed sometime last year.

"That eager to be rid of me?" His deep voice sounded a second before the door shut, and I suppressed a groan. Wheeler had a way of making me feel like the guilty party, when really, I steered clear of him because of his bad attitude and constant surliness.

"Eager to be back at home." As much as I wanted, no *needed*, to get laid, I wasn't sure The Barn Door was the right venue for me. I wasn't a prude, not by anyone's standards, but small town living was a big adjustment. I couldn't just get lost in the crowd and become anonymous. That meant I needed to be careful.

"I don't know what I was thinking going there, anyway."

Wheeler killed the engine and stepped from the SUV, tall and graceful, wide and purposeful. He walked like the whole army followed him. Always.

"You were thinkin' like everyone else in there. It'd be nice to get a good hard fuck in before the week starts up."

Pretty much. "Of course that's what you'd think." I scoffed.

He snorted and leaned against the hood. "There's no puttin' lipstick on that particularly slutty pig, sweetheart. But, hey, that's okay. I'm not judging."

No, he wasn't judging. He was mocking. Me. "Right. Well, good night Wheeler." I whirled on my heels, upset that I'd gone through the effort of getting dressed up in heels and sexy lingerie, all for nothing.

LOADED

"Aren't you gonna invite me up for a nightcap, Doc?"

His words stopped the movement of my feet instantly. I turned, slowly, to face him because I had to have misheard that tone. It sounded like he was inviting himself up for a bit of carnal exercise, but it couldn't be. Could it?

"You thirsty, Wheeler?"

His lips slowly curled up into a seductive smile, the kind that had blood slogging through my veins like lava, hot and thick. Dark with promise.

"I could go for a drink," he said.

I sucked in a deep breath and let it out slowly, counting to ten—hell, twenty—as goosebumps broke out all over my skin. If I invited him up, there was no mistake what would happen. I had no doubt in my mind it would be hot as hell. Satisfying. And a really, really bad idea. Wheeler had issues, but his issues weren't my problem. He wasn't trying to be my boyfriend. He wanted what I wanted. Physical release. And that decided it for me.

I took a step backwards and let a slow, hopefully seductive smile cross my face as I looked up at him. "Wheeler, would you like to come up for a nightcap?"

"I'd like that very much, Annabelle."

My legs felt stiff and also filled with liquid as I walked up the small blue wooden porch I'd repainted last summer. I shoved the first key and then the second, into the lock. Once the door opened and then closed, this would happen. I wanted it, I did. But I was still nervous and afraid.

The heat of Wheeler's body seeped into my already overheated frame. I took two steps beyond the threshold just to clear my head and slow my heart. Yeah, that was better. "What would you like to—"

Wheeler stepped inside and kicked the door closed with his big, booted foot.

"No more talking, Annabelle." Then his mouth was on mine, and I didn't give a damn about a nightcap or my nerves or whether this was a bad idea, because his mouth on mine was a good idea.

A *damn* good idea.

A moan slipped out of my mouth and into his, and Wheeler's big hands tightened on my hips. He sandwiched my body between his massive frame and the hard wall, a constant pressure that only accelerated my pulse even further.

"Yes," I moaned when his mouth moved from my mouth and down my jawline, then to my neck before his lips centered gently on my collarbone. "Oh, fuck, yes," I moaned.

He chuckled against my skin, the deep sound reverberated through my chest and back, intensifying the sexual high I had going on as his hands tangled in my thick brown hair.

"Annabelle." It came out as a soft growl and I tilted my head back, allowing him to capture my mouth again.

Then his hands began to move. Everywhere. Down my back, cupping my ass and resting on my hips. Then his rough fingers slid under my little black dress, fingertips playing along my hips, the waistband of my thong and then finally, the sensitive flesh at the swell of my breasts.

His touch was firm, slightly rough but somehow also inherently gentle. But I wasn't feeling so gentle as his big, rough hands quickly drove me out of my mind.

My hands went to the hem of his shirt and pulled it up and over his head, gasping at the visual of Wheeler without his shirt.

"Shit, you're beautiful," I thought his face, chiseled and rugged but unmistakably gorgeous was a masterpiece, but damn his torso nearly put it to shame. A dark smattering of hair covered his upper chest, light brown nipples playing peek-a-boo as the hair led down to a thick line that bisected an incredible abdomen, complete with scars, tattoos and a mouthwatering six pack.

LOADED

He let out a deep chuckle as his own hands moved lightning quick to remove my dress, and he stepped back to let his gaze roam over my body as thoroughly as a caress.

"I think you took the words right out of my mouth, Doc."

The way he spoke, his voice deep and thick with arousal, sent a bolt of lightning zipping through my body, so fierce I thought it might tear me apart. Wheeler was ready, mouth and hands slowly driving me out of my mind as I stood there, wrapped around his body in nothing but a bright red thong and black stilettos.

From there it was all frenetic movements of arms and legs, hands and mouths. Our bodies moved like they were possessed by pure, driven lust and nothing more. Wheeler kissed my neck and my shoulders as one hand slipped inside my panties until his middle finger found my pussy, wet and pulsing, rubbing slow, drugging circles around my clit.

"Wheeler," choked out of my throat.

I felt his grin a moment before that delicious tongue scraped across my nipple and pulled it into his mouth, sucking hard and letting his teeth sink into the sensitive skin just enough to sting but not hurt.

"So fucking sweet," he growled and put a hand to my wrist, stopping the progress I made on his button and zipper. "Not yet."

"Now," I told him because there was no way in hell I could wait, not with the way his fingers played my body like a master violinist. "Right. Now."

He let out a low growl, but I wasn't at all deterred, shoving his pants and boxers down to reveal his cock to me. "Yes."

He chuckled and grabbed my wrist again. "Annabelle." His voice held a warning but I couldn't hear it, not with the way my name rolled off his tongue. It only made me want him more.

"Wheeler," I said, just as determined as he was to have my way. I wrapped a hand around his cock, thick and long, maybe a full eight inches. Or maybe wishful thinking, either way, I wanted his cock. I wanted him.

Now.

My hand went to his chest and I pushed him against the other wall in my front hall, not caring at all when the photos fell to the floor. "No. More. Talking." I was done talking, my body was wound up too tight thanks to his thick, talented fingers and now all I wanted was that long, thick cock pounding into me.

I let my right hand slide down to cup his balls, and Wheeler rewarded me with a low, guttural groan.

"Fuck, Annabelle."

"Now you're getting it," I told him, and because I couldn't resist any longer, I dropped to my knees, getting a semi-good glance at his cock in the dim light of the front hall. It was long and thick, hard and throbbing, my mouth watering as I whispered, "Damn, Wheeler."

"You're good for my ego…Doc." The last word came out strained as I wrapped my lips around his cock, tasting every inch of him before I took him deep. "Oh fuck, Anna…shit."

I smiled around him and closed my eyes for several seconds, letting his grunts and moans act as the soundtrack to this encounter. He was longer than I thought, thicker too, and it turned me on even more, so I took him deeper and deeper still. He tasted good, like man and musk and sweat.

His hand reached out and sifted through my hair before he got a good handful of it, grabbing it just hard enough to send another wave of wetness between my thighs.

"Annabelle."

"Hmm?"

Those piercing blue eyes darkened at the vibrations and his lips twitched at the corners. "Enough."

"You sure? You seem…close."

"Too close," he bit out and helped me to my feet, walking down the hall as if he'd been here a thousand times before. "Perfect," he said when he spotted the dark green sofa. "That's where I wanna fuck you."

Yes, please. Maybe the devil took hold of me, or maybe it was just the innate masculinity oozing from Wheeler's pores calling out to me, but I stared at him for a minute and then the high arms of the sofa, then I looked back at him with a smile.

"Fuck, yeah." I leaned over the arm, legs wide and back arched to give him an excellent view of how soaked my panties were.

"Doc, you're fucking perfect." His pants were already halfway around his ankles so all I heard was the crinkle of a condom wrapper as he slid my panties to the side, and then a primal growl as his cock slowly entered me from behind.

"Oh fuck. Hot. Tight. Wet." He sank to the hilt and my eyes rolled into the back of my head as my hands white-knuckled the sofa.

"Yes, Wheeler." Something happened to my brain when he pulled out and pushed into me over and over again. The only two words I could seem to remember were his name and the word 'yes', moaning them over and over as he pounded into me, making me feel better than I had in a very long time.

Something felt like it snapped or changed in him, his strokes became less graceful, more frantic as if he was just as on edge as I was, clutching it tight to prolong the feeling. He stayed silent, focused on nothing but giving himself to me, giving me absolute pleasure from head to toe. Then his hips moved faster and faster, his legs trembled and his grip on my hips tightened, and a loud smack on my ass filled the air.

"Annabelle, fuck!"

The word came out on a roar as he pounded hard and fast into me, his own pleasure pouring out and igniting a fire that practically melted my veins. It was a combination of fire and an explosion, something I couldn't explain, only to say that it was powerful.

And dangerous.

LOADED

Pleasure coursed through my veins and then my body went limp against the sofa. Wheeler's found his orgasm and it stole his legs, adding more weight to my burden and something else.

Something cold. Hard. Something cold, hard and metal, attached to Wheeler's leg. Instantly I knew what it was. I could wonder how it happened. What the fuck it was, but in the moment, it didn't matter. What did matter was the aftershocks that tore through both of us. "That was...worth the trip to The Barn Door," I said on a breathless laugh.

Wheeler stood and pulled me up to my feet. "Damn. You gotta work on your compliments, Doc."

Ah, we were back to Doc again. I schooled my features and turned, keeping my eyes on his too good-looking face before letting them trail down his sweat-slicked body, hair mussed and his chest damp all the way down to his semi-hard cock. Still. And then I saw it, the prosthesis on his left leg, just below the knee. It was state of the art, black and chrome, probably lightweight considering I hadn't noticed over the past few months when my gaze would inevitably turn to him. But the way he held himself so straight and stiff, like he expected a negative reaction, told me a lot.

"Maybe I do," I told him and kicked off my stilettos. "Or maybe you'll earn a better compliment after round two."

His shoulders relaxed and he took a step forward, intent burning black in his eyes. "You know what, Annabelle?"

"What's that, Wheeler?"

"I like the way you think." And to prove it, he carried me to my bedroom and gave me round two, three and four before we both passed out in my king sized bed.

I wasn't the least bit surprised to find him gone when I woke the next morning.

Chapter One

Wheeler

Damn, the fists kept coming. First one to my side, which I was pretty fucking sure cracked a rib. Then came another, snapping my head back and sending blood rushing out of my nose.

"Motherfucker!" There was no way in hell I'd let it end like this, a bunch of anonymous, faceless pieces of shit who thought they could step up to me. That they could challenge me and live to talk about it. "I don't fucking think so."

The fucker's face was perfectly non-descript, exactly the way I tried to look whenever I was out in the field, trying to blend into whatever corner of the earth I'd been dropped in with my team. He had dark hair and dark eyes, no defining facial features. Yet. "Bring it, pretty boy!"

I couldn't wait to wipe that fucking smile off his face. I took a step forward with my left leg, digging it in as hard as I could and using that force to send my right fist slamming into the center of his face.

"Yeah, let's go motherfucker." That felt good. I hadn't been in a fist fight in a long time, not even with my family, the Reckless Bastards, and this felt good. Real fucking good.

The crack of my knuckles against the bone in that fucker's nose felt good and it felt even better when he cried out in pain and fell to his knees.

"You broke my nose," he said. His words were at odds with the smile on his face, which should've alarmed me, and it did.

Too fucking late. I felt the sharp, cool metal slide between a few ribs on my left side but I couldn't see the asshole behind me.

"You're dead, motherfucker!" I said.

I looked around and everything was dark. No, not just dark, pitch-fucking-black. I didn't know where I was or who the fuck I'd been fighting, and most of all, I had no fucking clue where my guys were.

"Yet, you're the one bleeding out," he whispered and stuck the knife in again, ducking when I turned with a spinning elbow. "Already too slow."

That was exactly what I hoped to hear from this dumb shit. "Maybe if I'd sucker stabbed you, we might be even." But I would delight in killing this asshole, whoever he was.

"Come on, GQ."

I didn't even bother responding or rolling my eyes. I'd heard it all before from pretty boy and GQ to Zach Morris and everything in between. "Aw, you think I'm hot? Thanks."

He frowned and came in for a jab that I easily dodged. A shot from his other hand grazed my shoulder, but it didn't affect me at all. Now he swung wildly, desperate to land something. Anything. I continued to dodge him, waiting for my moment, even as blood wet my shirt left and right. "You motherfucker, you're dead."

I smiled again and leaned back at another wild uppercut that nearly knocked him off balance.

"Bring it, you ugly piece of shit," I taunted. When he tried to correct his stance, he overcorrected and fell against me so all I had to do was wrap an arm around his neck.

"You done?"

"Fuck you," he spat and squirmed, but it was useless. The more he moved, the tighter my grip wrapped around him.

"I guess not," I laughed and pressed into this dipshit, making him even more uncomfortable, squirming even more.

"Let him go," his friend said, finally getting to his feet with a black gun aimed at my head.

"Fuck that." I wasn't afraid of a fucking gun, especially being held by a wannabe gangster.

"I said," he lifted the piece higher because clearly he had no fucking idea how guns worked. "Let. Him. Go."

"You want him?"

"You fuckin' heard me, didn't you?" the wannabe said.

I smiled. "I did." My smile slowly faded as the man barely squirmed, semi-conscious in my arms. With one hand on his cheek, I gave a quick jerk and he fell to the ground with a broken neck.

"Now you have him, asshole." I stepped over the limp body and stalked towards the other man who let off one shot, cracking me right in the kneecap, and I dropped to the concrete.

He lowered the gun, adjusting his aim with a mildly shaking hand. "You'll pay for that."

Somehow, I managed to stand and grab the gun from that asshole. "Maybe in another life." I emptied the clip into his chest and let him fall, stepping over him and heading to the sounds of traffic on the other end of the alley.

But another man appeared, charging at me. A quick throat punch sent him to the ground.

Another man came, and then another and another. They wouldn't stop, not even as hundreds of them bottle necked into the narrow alleyway.

There was no way I could fight them all, and I knew it. My adrenaline spiked and my heart was racing so hard I knew I'd pass out any second if I didn't get my shit under control. But the blows kept coming, hit after hit, and I felt my energy fading.

"Fuck," I panted and when I opened my eyes, they were gone.

No, not gone. They were never fucking there because I was in the bunkhouse on Hardtail Ranch. It was pitch black; the only sounds came from the crickets.

My heart was still racing, and my bed was soaked with sweat.

"Another fucking nightmare," I growled to the beams in the celling.

At least I was in here alone. No one to witness another humiliating nightmare. Lately, they'd been coming with more frequency. I should fucking recognize them and just wake the fuck up. But I never did. Not until it was too late.

Knowing I wouldn't get any more sleep before the sun came up, I swung my leg over the edge of the bed and rubbed my stump. It ached like a motherfucker, which explained the bullet to the knee. Goddamn dreams, they couldn't just be terrifying, could they? No, they also had to come with weird ass, hidden fucking messages that required a damn witch doctor to decipher. "Fuck!"

I didn't want to do it, didn't want to take another one of those fucking pills, but I needed it. No, I didn't need it, not if I wasn't going back to sleep and after that dream, I sure as shit wasn't.

With that settled, I grabbed my crutch and made my way to the bathroom, hoping a hot shower might wash away the memories and the pain of that fucking dream. It didn't work. Nothing ever fucking worked and despite what my brother Mitch thought, talking about it wouldn't help either.

I didn't need to talk. I needed fresh air. Fresh air and black coffee would erase just enough that I could make it through breakfast at the big house without drawing concerned stares from Holden and Peaches, and then through morning chores with Holden.

Cleaning up horse shit and wrangling cows wasn't as exciting as my old life, not even the MC had quite reached those levels yet, but it was a damn sight better knowing who I could trust and who was the enemy.

And so far, the Reckless Bastards hadn't cost me any goddamn limbs.

Chapter Two

Annabelle

Turning down the long winding dirt road that led to Hardtail Ranch, I let out a sigh and gripped the wheel just a little tighter than necessary. There was no reason to be nervous to go enjoy coffee and breakfast with one of the few friends I'd made outside of the hospital, yet here I was. Nervous.

And I knew why. Just one second after the big, gleaming white house came into view, so did a tall, brooding figure in the distance. Wheeler. I shouldn't be nervous or surprised to see him, but I was. I always was. And the worst of it was that even now, I couldn't look away. Even from a million miles away he was gorgeous and tall with broad shoulders, a narrow waist and well-muscled thighs that did dangerous things to denim.

He was the flame and I was the moth, doomed to burn my wings because I couldn't resist him. Even knowing all that, I ignored logic and reason when I stepped from my car and headed in the direction of Wheeler instead of what Peaches lovingly referred to as 'the big house.' Every step brought another deep breath and a small wish into the world that today he might closely resemble a pleasant human being.

"Little early for a fuck ain't it, Doc?"

So much for that hope. My shoulders fell in disappointment, and I cursed myself for even bothering to make the long walk over here. Wheeler was never happy to see me, which I didn't take too personally since he was never happy to see anyone. Still, it stung that he was happy to drop into my life and fuck me but couldn't be bothered to extend a little common courtesy.

But I always let him drop in and fuck me because he was hot and sexy and a damn good lay, but the way I felt about myself afterward was the exact opposite.

"I just came over to see how you were doing." It sounded pathetic even to my ears and his snort only confirmed it.

Wheeler turned to me, disdain written clearly in his beautiful sapphire eyes, darker and more intense in these early morning hours and even his dickish words hadn't diminished his effect on me.

"You don't need to worry about me. I'll be just fine." His words were confident and harsh, cold, intended to put more distance between us.

I should have just followed suit the first time he'd spoken to me like this and proved that I didn't mean anything to him, but I didn't. Instead I compounded the mistake I made three months ago when I invited him up for a drink and let him fuck me six ways from Sunday. I let my sympathy for him and his situation get in the way. Well, no more, dammit.

"So rude and cocky and arrogant," I huffed. "Especially for a man who can't get through the night without help from narcotics."

He sucked in a breath and glared at me *hard*, eyes saying so much while his mouth said nothing at all. He turned on his black leather-booted feet and walked away. I watched him until he faded from view and not once did he look back.

Not. Fucking. Once.

With a shrug, I turned in the direction of the big house and put Wheeler out of my mind. He was another in a long list of mistakes I'd made. Judging by the heat coursing through me, a mistake I'd probably make a few more times. By the time I reached the front steps, I'd pushed all thoughts of Wheeler into the deep recesses of my mind, slapped a small smile on my face and knocked as I pulled open the screen door. "Knock, knock! Anybody awake in here?"

"Back here, Belle." Peaches' nickname for me had my skin turning pink and my eyes rolling skyward. I had a love-hate relationship with the nickname because on the one hand it was pretty and delicate—which I wasn't—but on the other hand she said I reminded her of a very famous Belle which I did *not*. At all.

The kitchen was a bustle of activity, as it always was with Martha shuffling about making sure everyone had what they needed, putting buttery biscuits on the table and a plate stacked high with bacon. Maisie saw me first and slid off the wooden bench seat with a wide, toothless grin.

"Doctor Anna, hi!" She ran across the kitchen as fast as her little legs would carry her and slammed right into me. "I haven't seen you in forever."

I knelt down and scooped her up. "Forever huh? You haven't aged all that much in forever, honey."

That little gap between her front teeth melted my heart along with those big blue eyes and lopsided raven pigtails. "Not forever then," she rolled her eyes. "A really long time."

She was right, I hadn't been around much, only stopping in when someone needed stitching up, or when I was sure I wouldn't run into Wheeler. "Too many people have been getting scrapes and scars. It's kept me busy. How are you?" I squeezed her little body tight, loving the way she hugged back with her whole heart, so full of trust.

"Good. I can count money now, and Peaches and me are reading *Harry Potter*. You know it?"

"Do I know it? I have all the movies, kid. When you're done with the books, I'll let you borrow them, okay?"

She nodded and wiggled down to the floor as soon as Martha put the cinnamon rolls on the table. "Okay. Let's eat!"

Peaches laughed and helped the little girl back onto the bench, smiling at me as she nodded for me to sit. "Sugar beats everything, especially those buns."

"That's okay, I feel the same way about bacon cheeseburgers." I took the seat across from Peaches, trying to ignore the tension that between the two women. Martha had, inexplicably decided to continue working for Gunnar after her daughter was killed.

"Everything smells delicious, Miss Martha."

She beamed a rare smile at the compliment and set a hand on my shoulder. "Thank you, Dr. Keyes."

LOADED

"Annabelle, please." It was too late for her daughter, Adrian, by the time I'd arrived at the shootout, and all of my focus had been on Holden. I didn't understand why Martha decided to stay on the ranch.

"Thank you, Annabelle," Martha said reluctantly, yet giving me a smile. She set the eggs and hash browns on the table and beat a hasty exit from the kitchen. "How are things?" I asked Peaches as soon as Martha left.

She shrugged. "They are...what they are, I guess. She's quiet and withdrawn all the time but she claims she understands." Peaches shrugged again. I knew she was at a loss for how to get the peace back in her home, especially considering everything else going on.

"You believe her?"

She snorted. "Would you?"

I shook my head, aware of Maisie's little ears. "How could I? What does Gunnar have to say?"

"He feels guilty," she told me and that was all she needed to say.

"But he didn't..." There was only so much conversation we could have in the presence of a precocious kid with eager ears, so I didn't finish the sentence.

"No, it wasn't him," she said firmly, "but as the man in charge, he feels it all the same. Nothing I say changes that. He's stubborn."

I didn't know how she managed to trust Martha to cook their meals without slowly poisoning them or putting Maisie at risk, but it wasn't for me to understand. "All you can do is keep trying."

"Like you and your dad?"

I sighed and pushed the half-empty plate away from me. "No, not like that at all. This is nothing like that."

"You've been done with med school for how many years?" I knew what she was getting at with this line of conversation, and I hated it.

"Seven years since I finished and three since I completed my residency and fellowship. Why?"

She shrugged, turning her attention briefly to Maisie who'd finished breakfast and two cinnamon rolls and had now grown bored with adult conversation. They spoke quietly, hugged, and then Maisie trotted off to the living room, where some kid show blared from the speakers. "You know damn well why. Maybe in all the years since you last spoke, he's changed his mind."

"I called him when I got the fellowship at Johns Hopkins. He told me emergency medicine was a waste of my talents and his money." Peaches knew we hadn't spoken since.

"Does he know you're back in Texas?"

I shook my head and snagged the half eaten slice of cold bacon on my plate. "If he does, he didn't hear about it from me."

"So keep trying doesn't apply to you?"

"There's nothing to try. Gunnar's guilt is misplaced. He did the right thing and feels bad because he is a good man. My father is upset I chose to do something other than follow the path he wanted for me. There's no changing that." I couldn't keep someone in my life that made me feel like a constant disappointment, and I'd told her as much. "It's a pattern I've worked hard to break, and I won't go back for anyone. Not even him."

"Fine," she said on a sigh. "I'll keep trying with Gunnar because I love him and I'll keep trying to get you to change your mind about your dad because he's your dad."

"No, he's my father and there's a difference." I knew she wanted to argue with me, and I shook my head. "I know why you think it's important, Peaches, but it isn't the same."

She sighed. "Fair enough. I can't put my lack of daddy issues on you. That's not fair."

"Thank you." With that topic beaten to death, we both fell into a contemplative silence.

LOADED

The comfortable quiet was disturbed by heavy footsteps stomping up the back stairs. The screen door yanked open as Wheeler entered, bringing nothing but noise and chaos with him. A complete and total disturbance.

"Mornin'," he grunted, I assumed at Peaches and kept my mouth shut.

"Hey, Wheeler, how's it going today?" Her gaze stayed on me, determined and insistent while I pretended not to notice.

He shrugged and filled an oversized mug with black coffee. "It'll be going a lot better when this damn headache is gone."

"Talk to him," she mouthed the words to me, and I shook my head. There was no way in hell that I would get in the middle, *more* in the middle of Wheeler and the issues he clearly planned to ignore until they destroyed him. "Maybe you need water?"

He glared at her, but she kept that sweet smile trained on him until his shoulders relaxed and most of his attitude dissipated. "Water lacks caffeine, smart ass."

She shrugged, not at all put off by his tone. "Caffeine dehydrates you which causes headaches. But hey, you keep doing you, Wheelie." Her words held a bit more bite, and she turned back to me, annoyance spread all over her face.

"I will." He grunted and left, sucking most of the air out of the room and not sparing one damn glance for me.

"Anna, talk to him. Please."

"No." It was as simple as that, for so many reasons. "I practice emergency medicine, Peaches. A few rotations in the psych department doesn't make me an expert."

"Maybe not, but it's clear he's suffering and needs help."

I nodded my agreement. Wheeler was in a world of pain, both physical and mental, and I was pretty sure no one on the ranch knew how much. But he wasn't my patient. Hell, he wasn't my anything. "He has to want help first, Peaches."

"I hate that," she said with a pout that made her look more like Maisie than the fully capable woman I knew her to be. "He's so clearly hurting."

He was hurting more than she knew, and even though Peaches was my closest friend, it wasn't my place to tell Wheeler's tale. "So, how was New York?"

Peaches shrugged. "Uneventful." It wasn't exactly a non-answer, but I got the distinct impression Peaches just lied to me and didn't want to talk about it.

KB WINTERS

Chapter Three

Wheeler

"What the hell crawled up your ass, man?" Holden's deep voice sounded behind me, startling me out of my own damn thoughts. I whirled on him.

"Don't sneak up on me, dude. We've talked about this." He wore a smirk that I wanted to punch off his smug damn face. Just because he was all happy and in love, getting laid on a regular fucking basis, didn't mean he needed to rub it in everyone's face. "Unless you'd like to get your ass kicked again."

Holden wasn't offended at all. Instead he tossed his head back and laughed. And laughed. It went on so long I started to get pissed off. It wasn't that goddamn funny. "You got one sucker punch on me, man. Let's not exaggerate."

"You snuck up on me, that's not a sucker punch. It's self-defense." He should know that better than anyone.

"Not if I called your name half a dozen times before laying a hand on your fucking shoulder." Holden shook his head, sympathy and irritation shining in his eyes. "Get your shit together Wheeler. You're the VP and we're all counting on you."

"A little early for a guilt trip, isn't it? Didn't even pack my earplugs." Yeah, I was being a dick, and I knew it, but I was damn sick of everyone treating me like some fucking head case.

"Be a dick if you want but listen. We all went through shit in the service. You've done, seen, and gone through more than the rest of us combined, but look at you." He waved one of his big meaty hands in my direction, and I folded my arms, expression defiant. "You're clearly not sleeping through the night, can't be bothered to shave, and you've been out here by these fucking fences all day. Thought maybe you'd passed out in the sun."

A frown crossed my face, and I whipped out my phone to glance at the time. "Shit." Holden was right, dammit. I'd missed lunch and the day was nearly over, but the fence I should've been mending wasn't even close to finished. "Sorry, man. I'll get it done, don't worry about it." This was all the Doc's fault, damn her. The last thing I needed to see after a restless night was her face, all beautiful and earnest and concerned.

About me.

Fuck that.

I didn't need her concern, what I needed and what I wanted, was her body. I loved to fuck Annabelle, loved the way she wrapped that sexy body around me and gripped me tight like she couldn't let me go. I loved the way she looked in those red-framed glasses when she dropped to her knees and sucked me off. It was an intoxicating blend of innocence and sex appeal. Something I never thought I wanted until I came upon the Doc looking scared and intrigued about the pleasures found inside The Barn Door.

Since then, we'd fuck on a regular basis, usually when I dropped by the cute little bungalow she lived in. And yeah, maybe those times lined up with my need for a few extra painkillers, but we didn't talk about that. Or the worried brown eyes she always laid on me when I asked. I didn't need the worry, I needed the Oxy so I could sleep without the fucking dreams that were never the same but they were always exhausting.

Getting lost in her body was one of my favorite past times, but I hated that she knew all about my nightmares and especially hated that she knew about my leg.

Those were *my* secrets dammit, and I was grateful that she took her job as a physician seriously, because none of the Reckless Bastards knew my secrets. Only Annabelle and Mitch.

"You don't have to do this shit by yourself, Wheeler." Holden was still upset, but I was starting to get the idea that it wasn't about the damn fence.

"What the fuck is your problem, then?"

"You are, asshole!" He pushed me and not gonna lie, it shocked the fuck out of me because Holden was the quiet one. The one who took his time before acting. Or *re*acting.

"We are supposed to be a family but you, Wheeler, are a fucking island."

"Don't give me that," I told him, struggling to hold on to my own calm. "I'm here aren't I? Have been every step of the way, every fucking fight I've been there, stepping in the shit to make sure we all make it home safe." It was no different than my time in the service.

"Yeah and that's great, but what about you? It's clear there's some shit going on with you, and you look like hell. How can any of us trust you to have our backs when you don't trust none of us with what's going on with you?"

"I'm fine, Holden. Sometimes I have trouble sleeping and when that happens I'm a surly asshole, what can I say?"

"You're always a surly asshole," he shot back, a tiny smile cracking through his scowl. "But we both know it's more than that."

"I'm fine," I insisted the same way I did when Mitch got on my case about seeing a professional.

"Talking to some headshrinker won't change a fucking thing, Holden."

"Have it your way," he growled and walked away, hopping on the caramel-colored gelding and riding off into the literal fucking sunset.

Left alone with my thoughts, they inevitably turned back to the things giving me the most trouble. Annabelle and my goddamn nightmares. They were so linked, and at this point, I couldn't think of one without the other. The dreams were always the same, fighting an enemy with more men and resources than I had until they overwhelmed me.

And the only thing that could come close to soothing them was Annabelle.

And the pills.

I didn't have either right now so I turned back to the fence and worked until my muscles screamed in pain, and I was too damn tired to think about anything or anyone.

Chapter Four

Annabelle

"Got any fun plans tonight, Annabelle?" Nurse Peyton's wide, beaming smile flashed at me in the semi-lit parking lot of the hospital.

I snorted and shook my head as we both stepped off the curb and headed to our separate cars. "Exactly the opposite. I plan to read a few journal articles, maybe pop a load into the laundry and find something that's not a sandwich for dinner. Jealous?"

Her laugh was as contagious as her smile. "You bet your perky little butt I am. I have three kids with homework to do and dinner to eat, one husband out of his depth and probably an entire house that needs to be cleaned. Your night sounds like a dream." She flashed a big grin that underscored her words and proved she was as in love with her life as I thought she was. "Wanna trade?"

That pulled another laugh from me. "I wouldn't know how to even get kids into bed, Tish. Give me a wound to stitch, blood and guts, and I'm far more comfortable."

She laughed. "It all seems scary at first. Then you jump right in and take control, just like in the ER." She sounded so sure and so certain that I almost believed her. Almost.

"Says the woman who wrangles kids with the same ease she does cowboys and rangers." It was a talent I admired and one of the reasons I always requested her on my service.

"It's a gift, what can I say? But it would be nice to have a quiet night on my own once in a while." She laughed and aimed the key fob in the direction of her car, making both sets of light flash. "We always want what we can't have, don't we?"

"I don't know, Tish, it sounds like a great idea."

She waved away my words with a grin. "Don't you worry about all that, Doc. I'll be just fine."

LOADED

"Of course you will, but it's totally selfish on my part. You're my best nurse, and I can't stand it when you're not here." I said.

She rolled her eyes and tossed her oversized bag into the backseat. "That's hardly the truth but thank you all the same. Have a good night, Doc."

"You too, Tish. Hug those adorable boys for me, if they let you close enough."

Her laughter echoed in the night. "Only if I promise to regale them with tales of blood and guts in the ER. Which I won't." She shivered. "Why the Good Lord punished me with a house full of boys, I'll never know."

She loved each and every one of her boys and all of Opey knew it. The boys, along with her husband Daryl stopped by often during double shifts with dinner, drawings, and snacks simply because they missed her. I'd be lying if I said I wasn't a little bit envious, but more than that, Tish gave off this sense of maternal affection that was hard to resist. "Who else could handle them better?"

She grinned and tossed a wave my way before closing the door and driving off. A few minutes later, I headed in the opposite direction towards my little bungalow. The proximity to the hospital was the main reason I'd chosen the house, along the dead-end street that provided endless hours of peace and quiet.

I turned onto my block, lined with just seven houses, three on each side and one bigger house at the end. The block was quiet, just the way I liked it, with only the crickets providing a soundtrack and lightning bugs providing ambience. But all the peace that had quickly settled over me vanished when I turned into my driveway and noticed a familiar figure sitting on my front porch.

Wheeler had his legs stretched out in front of him, crossed at the ankles, his elbows resting on the top step and his head tilted towards the night sky, a small smile playing on his lips. He almost looked normal, not tortured or angry or surly. Almost.

Whatever he was feeling right now was irrelevant to me. I'd had a long shift that started at four o'clock this morning, and I wasn't in the mood for his attitude. I gave myself one quick look in the rearview mirror, let out a sharp breath and stepped out into the cool night air. Wheeler didn't move but his gaze went from the sky to my approaching form. There was heat and appreciation in his gaze and even though my body started to respond as I got closer, my mind squashed that nonsense.

"Evenin', Doc."

"Not tonight, Wheeler. I'm not in the mood."

One of the boards creaked when he stood, and I felt the heat of his body right behind me as I fumbled with my keys.

"Really?" His deep voice rumbled and sent a shiver straight down my spine. "Fifty bucks says I could change your mind."

Of course, that was what he thought. Finally, the key found the hole, and I shoved my door open, stepping inside to face him.

"Fuck you, Wheeler. I'm not in the mood for you."

He blinked. Stunned. I was probably the first woman in a very long time to turn him down, and like a man who looked, well how Wheeler looked, he was speechless. "Since when?"

Seriously? "Since. Right. Now." I was starting to remember exactly why it had been more than a year since I'd had sex before that night, those months ago. "I've been at work and it's almost nine, Wheeler. I don't have the time, energy, or patience for your shit tonight."

"Come on, Doc. Don't be like that." He stepped in close enough that his scent invaded my space and my senses, making my nipples harden and my belly clench tight. "We always have a good time. Don't we?"

Despite my body's reaction to this man, my brain was fully in charge right now. Well, *not* fully because I had worked nearly seventeen hours today but in charge enough that I wouldn't cave, wouldn't give in to this tempting man.

"In bed, sure. But I'm tired. Too tired." My words were firm despite the fact that my body vibrated with need for him. "Good night." I stepped back to close the door and his big hand flew out, the leather cuff barely an inch from my face.

"Doc, wait." His voice had lost its playful tone. His blue eyes were serious now, so dark they appeared black in the dim light of the porch and the front hall.

Suddenly it all became clear. "Right. Of course." He wasn't here to see me or fuck me, he was here for him. "If you want more pills you'll have to come into the hospital like everyone else, Wheeler." He more than qualified to get his painkillers on the up and up, and so he would have to from now on.

"I didn't say that."

"You didn't have to; I'm not an idiot." At least not in the traditional sense, yet everything I'd done since I started sleeping with this man said otherwise. "I don't keep any medicine here. Come in tomorrow afternoon, and I'll get you set up."

A low growl came from deep in his belly, and I took a step back, making Wheeler frown. "You afraid of me now?"

"No. What part of tired do you not understand, or is it that you think I don't work hard all day?"

"I never said that," he began, raking a big hand through thick chestnut waves. "I just don't get what's changed."

"Maybe I'm sick of being used, Wheeler. Maybe I'm sick of letting you into my home, my bed only for you to turn around and act like an asshole. I've never asked a damn thing of you, other than basic human decency and that seems too much. So if you want pills, come to the hospital or find another source. Good night."

I slammed the door in his face and leaned against it while my heart raced so loud it was all I could hear for several minutes. It felt good, but I also felt like a garbage human being for turning away a man, a patient, so clearly in need.

But he was using me.

His large hand landed on the door but it wasn't threatening or even angry, it was almost an anguished pat. "Annabelle, let me in. Please." His arrogant, commanding tone was gone and my heart went out to him.

"Dammit, Wheeler. Why are you doing this?" My voice was barely above a whisper, but he heard me.

"Because as much as I hate it, you know the truth. About the nightmares and the pain." Of course he chose this moment, when I wanted to be alone, to be brutally honest.

"I'm having trouble sleeping."

"The nightmares again?"

"Again. Still. However you want to put it." All the arrogance had fled and in its place there was just pain and vulnerability remaining.

Even though I knew about the nightmares, had witnessed them just once, I wasn't crazy enough to believe him so easily. "I'm sorry to hear that, but I don't have anything here Wheeler."

"You're here," he said simply as if that meant something to me.

"This is my house, where else would I be?"

"Let me in, Annabelle. Please. I'll keep my hands to myself."

I snorted even though my hand was already curled around the doorknob and my other hand was poised on the deadbolt lock.

"Fine," he said, the smile returned to his voice now that he knew he was *this close* to getting his way. "I promise to try, very fucking hard, to keep my hands to myself."

That was a more believable promise, at least that's what I told myself as I opened the door. "Come in."

He smiled, and I looked away because it was too powerful, too potent to look at directly without falling at his feet. It was like his superpower, and he knew it, based on the way his smile brightened when I turned back to him. "Thanks."

"Sure." It wasn't like I could, in good conscience, turn away a person in need. Especially when that person was working very hard to make it seem like he wasn't in pain. I understood and sympathized with his pain, and I appreciated the sacrifices he'd made for the sake of the country.

"Make yourself at home, Wheeler." I kicked off my shoes, and he grabbed my hand, helping to keep me balanced. "Thanks."

"Where are you going?"

"Upstairs to shower and then find some kind of sustenance. Is that all right with you?"

He dropped my hand like it burned him, those blue eyes dimmed just a bit, the laughter disappeared completely. "Yeah. Sorry."

Dammit. He was really hurting, and I was a bitch. It didn't help at all that my behavior was justified, because pain radiated from every inch of his six-four frame. "It's all right. Go sit down and watch some television, I'll be down in a bit."

"Don't hurry on account of me, Doc. You're doing me the favor here." Even though I expected it, his return to the arrogant veneer he preferred stung like a bitch.

No good would come from confronting Wheeler, he was too fucked up. I turned away and climbed the steps to my bedroom and took my time.

Prolonging the inevitable.

Chapter Five

Wheeler

As soon as I heard the Doc's bedroom door close, I headed for the kitchen in search of a beer. I shouldn't have come here, dammit. I didn't want to put up with her shit any more than she clearly didn't want to put up with mine.

But here I was and not because I wanted pills. Painkillers were nice because I could sleep without the crazy fucking dreams and wake up with minimal pain. As long as I stayed on top of it, pills kept the phantom pain from getting too bad. But this time, I was here because of Annabelle. Something about the pretty little doctor kept me calm, helped me sleep.

Most of the time.

But she was right, I was an asshole to her—always—and she didn't deserve it. She'd been serving as the MC's unofficial doctor, stitching us up and yanking bullets out of us without asking questions, even though she had to have at least a million of 'em. That was another damn thing I liked about her, which just pissed me off. Dr. Annabelle Keyes was not a woman I could or should like. She was a professional, a doctor, and she probably had dreams of picket fences, a loving husband and even an eager border collie greeting her every night after work. That wasn't me, not by a long shot.

Still, she let me in when she didn't want to. I grabbed one of those expensive craft beers she favored with the funky labels and noticed food she clearly planned to cook tonight. It was the least I could do and the sight of that big juicy steak along with broccoli, bell peppers, an onion, and carrots made me realize I hadn't eaten since breakfast at the main house.

I didn't know what she planned to make, but I'd done enough kitchen duty in the military, mostly as punishment for stepping out of line in my younger years, that I could whip up something for both of us. Her expensive beer went down smooth. It was icy and hoppy and slightly bitter. Damn good, even if it did cost three times what plain old Budweiser did.

"What do you think you're doing?"

She caught me at the stove, seasoning meat, flipping vegetables, and filling her kitchen with incredible smells.

I smiled at her indignant tone before turning to flash her what Peaches called my panty melting smile, but I was the one surprised, again, by how fucking beautiful she was. It wasn't an over the top, in your face kind of beauty either. It was simple and unassuming. But damn beautiful.

Her hair was still damp and hanging down her back, clinging to her pale skin, slightly pink from the hot shower. She wore a green and white t-shirt that dropped down to mid-thigh, giving the appearance she wore nothing underneath. I knew it was a lie, but my cock didn't, or maybe he didn't care. Maybe my cock was just intrigued by the length of smooth, shapely legs on display.

Neither me nor my cock gave a damn that with her crossed arms and the pissed off expression on her face, she wouldn't be letting me see what actually was underneath that t-shirt.

"Has it been that long since a man cooked for you, Doc?" It was another asshole thing to say, but I really just couldn't seem to help myself around her.

She snorted and rolled her eyes. "I don't need a man to do for me what I am perfectly capable of doing for myself."

Ah, I knew she had a mile-wide independent streak, and I knew how to get her good and riled up. "Not everything," I said with a condescending grin because dammit I loved to spar with her.

"Everything," she said with attitude, her expression serious and unamused.

Maybe this was why I liked being around her and being an asshole to her. "Surely not everything, Doc." My voice was low and seductive, and hell yeah I was flirting with her, trying to entice her into helping me break my promise to keep my hands to myself. Too bad she wasn't biting. Not yet, anyway.

"There's *nothing* a man can do to or for you, better than you can?"

She sighed and dropped her arms, giving me a glimpse of two hard-tipped nipples that she couldn't hide from me. "In the moment, sure. But when I give myself an orgasm it comes with no drama. No demands. And no bullshit."

Those clear brown eyes said so much, and I heard it loud and clear, she considered me one of those people who brought drama and demands.

"Good thing I'm keeping my hands to myself then, isn't it?"

"Very."

I loved it when she got all prissy because it was a show. It was all bullshit. I saw how her pulse fluttered when my voice pitched low, and I remember exactly how she liked to be fucked. Hard and rough. She was insatiable and dirty. Just how I liked my women.

"So, what's for dinner?" she asked.

I smiled again because of how hard she was working to ignore the heat that sizzled between us. It was fine, I'd play her game for now. "Stir fry, I guess. You had all these damn vegetables and that weird teriyaki sauce so that's what I made."

"Thanks. That was…thoughtful."

"I'll try not to be too offended that you sound so damn surprised I can be thoughtful."

She shrugged like it didn't matter whether I was offended or not, and her being so standoffish made me want her more.

"Since I've seen no evidence of your thoughtful side, surprise is warranted." Luckily, she had a great pair of legs, and I was barely listening as she walked to the fridge and bent over, giving me a glorious view of her heart shaped ass—in tiny white shorts that cupped her ass like a glove—and came out with a beer.

LOADED

"So, want to talk about what's bothering you?" Leaning against the fridge with one foot crossed over the other, she looked as calm as could be.

I glared at her, hard, but I wasn't shocked by her boldness. "Nope." Instead of explaining or waiting for her next line of questioning, I started to put the rice, vegetables and steak strips on plates for each of us, walking carefully to the table and back so she wouldn't notice my painful limp because the last damn thing I needed was sympathy.

Her sympathy.

I felt her gaze on my body and this time it wasn't a caress or appreciation, it was medical. Impersonal. I braced myself for the upcoming lecture, something she and my brother, Mitch, fucking excelled at.

After watching me for too damn long, Annabelle pushed off the fridge and tucked the beer bottle into the crook of her arm, grabbing her plate in one hand and the napkin and flatware in the other before she marched out of the kitchen. Without a word.

"What the hell, Doc?" I grabbed my plate and followed her, slower because of the pain in my leg. When I reached the living room, I scowled at her, already curled up on one end of the sofa with her legs tucked under her and a small wooden tv tray already set up, remote in her hand while she browsed movies and TV shows.

"Why did you leave like that?"

She shrugged but her gaze never left the screen mounted on the wall. "You show up here, uninvited, and you don't want to talk. We're not having sex, and I have no drugs, what else do you want if not to talk to someone?" She browsed a few more channels while I stared at her numbly. "Should I get in your face and force you to tell me what brought on the nightmares?"

"No," I grunted out.

"Glad we're in agreement. Sit and eat, or don't." She shrugged again, finding some movie where people were singing and dancing with a smile, before she tucked into her food. "It's good, thanks."

LOADED

I took the seat on the other end of the sofa, taking my signal from Annabelle who was content to eat in silence while she got lost in the silly singing and dancing on the screen. A full hour passed with the only sound being forks on plates and a bunch of homeless artists singing about not having enough money to pay their bills. It wasn't bad but it was damn depressing. "You got nothing to say?" Why her silence pissed me off, I couldn't say. I should've appreciated that she wasn't pushing me to tell her all my shit. But I didn't.

And I hated to be ignored.

When her plate was empty and there was no threat our conversation would ruin her meal, she pushed the small tray table away and turned to me, legs still tucked under her body. "You're a grown man Wheeler. You've led men into war and you tend to cattle or whatever it is you do on the ranch. If you wanted to talk then I assume you would."

I both appreciated that and hated the fuck out of it. "I guess."

Her sigh spoke of her annoyance, and she reached for her beer, groaning at the empty bottle. I watched her curiously as she stood, grabbed her plate and left for the kitchen, returning moments later with another beer. Annabelle tucked herself back into the corner and turned those big, all-seeing brown eyes on me. "What branch of the military were you in?"

"That's what you want to know?" Most women wanted to know if I killed any terrorists and if so, how many. I didn't peg her as that kind of woman, but I'd been wrong before.

"No. I want to know what's causing the nightmares and the pain, but since you don't want to talk about that, tell me about the military."

"I was in the Army. Special Forces."

Her eyes widened slightly like she was surprised or maybe even impressed. "Like Green Berets?"

I nodded. "Some people still call us that, but we stick with special forces since it encompasses much more than our headgear." It wasn't an offensive term, just a very basic description of who the public thought we were.

"Why the Army?" Her questions were thoughtful and the way she rested her beer on one knee and her chin in her hand told me she was genuinely interested in the answer.

"Why not?" It was my prepared answer but Annabelle just stared as if she knew there was more to it. "Wasn't a strong swimmer until I got to the Army and honestly, the recruiter made it sound cool as shit. Plus, they offered to pay for the rest of my education."

"You were in college when you joined? That doesn't happen often does it?"

"Not that I know of, but I had no way to pay for college without going deep in debt, which would have been fine if I'd had a clue about what I wanted to do with my life."

She nodded thoughtfully. "Did the military help you figure it out?"

I snorted. "Obviously not. All I got was a shit ton of nightmares and half a goddamn leg."

"So you regret your service?"

"Hell no. I did a lot of fucking good for my country, and I'll never regret that. It just didn't turn out how I thought it would." My heart clenched even as I thought about it, about the hot shit smartass I'd been in my younger years, dreaming that I'd be something important. Somebody important.

"Thank you for your service, and your sacrifice Wheeler."

She stunned me once again. Those soft, sincere words hit me square in the chest and made me feel warm and uncomfortable. Why the fuck did she have to be so fucking sweet? So goddamn appealing? And why, for the love of all that's holy in this world did her pink lips and those red glasses make her look like every naughty librarian fantasy I'd ever had come to life?

"Sure," I grunted and hoped she'd change the conversation before I went back on my promise to her.

Her lips curled into a very small smile, like I amused her. "Did you do a lot of super secret missions?"

I nodded and waited for her to ask for details I couldn't give. "I did."

Again with that thoughtful nod, only this time she also took a long pull from her beer. "You've seen a lot of fucked up shit, probably done more than your fair share too."

"Your point?"

She didn't let my tone bother her. That realization made her more appealing to me but also made me more uncomfortable. "My point is that your nightmares make sense, even though that doesn't help you at all."

No shit. "What about you? Why'd you become a doctor?" If she wanted to get personal, two could play that game.

She shrugged and changed her position on the sofa so her legs were extended across the sofa just inches from my legs. Her bare feet arched in my direction, and she took a sip from her bottle. "My father's a doctor. So I guess you could say it's the family business. But I wanted to help people, and he encouraged me."

"What about your mom, was she a doctor too?" I wondered if she came from a wealthy family who turned the seasons into verbs and traced their lineage to the Mayflower and shit like that.

"My mom died when I was six years old and all I remember of her are photos."

"I lost my dad at a young age too. It fucking sucks."

Her lips twitched and big brown eyes burned with gratitude. "It does," she agreed with a huff.

"Your dad must be proud as shit though, right? My own mom hated the idea of the military especially since I was already in college, but she came around. Eventually."

"He is proud to an extent," she explained with what could only be described as a heavy heart. "But he believes I'm wasting my talents as an emergency surgeon. Dad works as a cardio-thoracic surgeon at Houston Methodist, so he's a little biased."

"Shit, even I'm impressed." She glared at me, hard, telling me just what she thought of that sentiment. "But he must be a real asshole if patching people up when they're on the brink of death isn't good enough. Hell, if not for people like you, most of us wouldn't have made it back alive." Combat medics were the reason I still had some leg left and why I hadn't died of an infection.

"He is who he is, and I love him, but we aren't close."

Which meant she had no one, just like me. Except I had the Reckless Bastards.

"Does that mean you'll be at the ranch for the holidays?"

She laughed. "It means I'll probably work so my colleagues can spend the holiday with their families."

Of course she thought about everyone else, because that was just who she was. She'd shown up time and again to stitch up me or one of the other guys in the MC. Making sure they were healthy and safe without getting the law involved.

"You're too good to be true, Doc."

She snorted a laugh that should've been unattractive but it wasn't. She was beautiful and the fact that she didn't try made her even more so. "Enough talking, Wheeler. Relax. Try to stop thinking so much about…every damn thing."

Her words made me grin, and I shook my head. Yep, she was definitely too good to be true. "If you insist." I set my plate on the coffee table and kicked off my shoes before stretching my body across the length of the sofa so my feet hung off one end and my head rested in her lap. "Better?"

"Shhh," she said and slowly sifted her fingers through my hair until it was impossible to keep my eyes open.

Chapter Six

Annabelle

A sound woke me, and I blinked several times trying to figure out where I was and how I'd gotten there. The television was still on, playing some old movie from the eighties, and I knew I was at home, but the feel of a hot, heavy arm across my midsection startled me fully awake. I tried to get up but the hand tightened, and a familiar, leather and sandalwood blend hit my nostrils.

Wheeler.

Wheeler, who had somehow managed to make me see him as more than a random biker with a bad attitude. He was a man. A veteran. A brother. And the things he'd shared with me forced me to see him as a whole human being and not just a cock to ride when the mood struck, when things in the ER got a little too real. It was the last damn thing I wanted, to have sympathy for the insufferable man, but when the mild moaning began, I was powerless to stop my heart from breaking just a little on his behalf.

"No. Stop. I don't know." The moaning, that was what woke me up which meant the nightmare was just starting.

"Wheeler, wake up." I kept my voice soft and soothing, the tone gentle the same way I did when a big strong man came in and needed stitches. "Wheeler."

"No, goddammit!" The moans grew louder and the anguish was almost a living breathing thing in the room. The pain in his voice was palpable.

"Wheeler it's all right. It's just a nightmare, none of it's real." My hand went to his leg, rubbing up and down from his hip to his knee. "Wheeler, wake up."

"Stand the fuck down!" His voice roared into the quiet living room, panic evident. "Take cover!"

"Wheeler!"

He sat up straight, nearly knocking me off the sofa before he opened his eyes. "Doc?"

"Yep, it's me," I said, my shoulders slumping in relief. "You okay?"

"Yeah," he said on a low, guttural sigh. Wheeler's voice was gritty and scratchy as he dropped back down on the sofa. "Just fucking fine, Annabelle."

I ignored the shiver that stole through me at the way he'd said my name and squirmed to get free of his grasp. He was feeling surly and probably more than a little embarrassed that I'd witnessed him in a vulnerable position, but Wheeler kept his grip on my waist tight. "Where ya going?"

"To bed. Feel free to sleep right here while you can. Down here," I said one more time just in case he thought about changing the rules. Again. I had to bite back a groan when he pulled my back flush against his chest and his cock because goodness, the man was big and hard. Everywhere.

"What do you think you're doing?" I knew, and I felt my body giving in so my only hope was that my brain would intervene before things got out of hand.

Wheeler held me close and whispered in my ear, his lips brushing the shell of my ear with every syllable. "I tried Annabelle. I really fucking tried." Before I could ask what he'd tried to do, his mouth was on mine, and I knew.

This was decision time. Would I give in to the shivers breaking out all over my skin as his mouth devoured mine? Or, would I push him away, denying us both what was destined to be a spectacular fuckfest? When his tongue slipped between my lips I knew the decision had already been made. I kissed Wheeler back, climbing on top of him like a monkey in a tree and wrapped my arms around his neck to deepen the kiss. When he moaned into my mouth and grabbed my hips, I started to grind against him, feeling the hard ridge of his denim-covered cock right where I wanted him.

No, needed him. "Wheeler," I panted as I pulled back, grabbing my t-shirt and pulling it over my head.

"Yeah," he bit out as his hands slid up my hips to my waist and over my ribcage before those big, calloused hands cupped my tits. His eyes were unfocused as they settled on my chest, thumbs and forefingers lightly pinching my nipples.

"You made a valiant effort," I told him playfully and arched into his touch. "Have a taste as your reward." My own words were rewarded with a deeply masculine growl as he leaned forward and swiped a tongue over one hard nipple and then another. "Yes."

My head fell back, and I closed my eyes, reveling in the way he grunted and growled with every swipe of his tongue, each time his teeth nipped into my tits. Wheeler was a man who didn't have sex, he didn't make love. He fucked. He fucked hard and fast and wild, and it was exactly why I couldn't get enough of him.

Asshole.

"Such sweet fucking tits, I wonder if I put in enough effort if I could make you come just by suckin' on 'em."

"It'd be worth a try," I told him on a breathless moan. "For the sake of science and all."

"Right," he bit the word out, sharp and harsh before leaning in again and sucking a nipple hard. So hard my eyes watered even as I arched into him, feeding the breast to him because I was a greedy bitch and I wanted it all. I wanted everything.

Then his hands were on the move, sliding up my thighs until he reached the bottom of my shorts and his fingers slipped under the lightweight cotton until he found my pussy, wet and swollen. All because of him. My gasp of pleasure sent a satisfied smile dancing across his face.

"Your pussy is always so damn wet."

I laughed. "That happens when you play with her…oh!" One long thick finger slipped inside and my back arched on its own even as I slid closer, needing to feel more of him.

"Fuck, Wheeler." His mouth was on my tits again even as his finger plunged in and out of me while I rocked against him, every other touch sending his knuckles brushing against my clit. "Wheeler," I moaned.

LOADED

I felt good. Damn good. But it wasn't good enough and I tried to back away but he held me close. "Not yet." To make his point, one strong hand held my hip while the other continued to strum my pussy like he was Jimi Hendrix, sending my pleasure up and up until I couldn't fight him any longer.

"I want to see your face when you come, Annabelle. I want to feel the way your cunt tightens, ah just like that," he groaned with a seductive smile, "when you're close. The way your pussy leaks like a faucet when your orgasm is close."

Goodness, his dirty words only made my pussy wetter and my nipples harder.

"Wheeler."

"You hear that?" Two fingers plunged in and out of my pussy, the only sound besides my heavy breathing was the outrageously slick sound of Wheeler fingering me. "I love that fucking sound because it means soon, I get to see you fall apart." Then he gave himself exactly what he wanted, and what I wanted.

"Oh holy fuu-uuck!" The orgasm barreled out of me like a tornado, whirling and tearing me apart inch by inch, while I shook and convulsed in his arms. I was vaguely aware of his words but the orgasm was long and eventually, I fell limp against his chest.

"That was...a good start."

"Good? Now I know you're full of shit, sweetheart." Sweetheart was better than Doc but it was still a way to keep himself apart, which normally didn't bother me. I didn't want to think too hard about why it did, so I slid off his lap, moaning as his fingers slipped free.

"Too. Many. Clothes." I was still breathless from the force of the orgasm. He grinned a satisfied smile as he tore off his shirt and tossed it aside.

"Better?"

Hell yeah it was. Wheeler, in his uniform of jeans, a plain t-shirt and his motorcycle boots was already mouthwatering and panty melting, but without his clothes on? He was pretty fucking god-like. It wasn't just his much too gorgeous face with the sharp cheekbones and pouty pink lips bracketed by a strong, stubbled jawline. It was the whole damn package, the perpetually mussed chestnut brown hair, the honeyed skin from too many hours shirtless on the ranch, the tattoos that barely distracted from the scars at his side, on his back and chest.

"Much better, but you could have on less." Last time it was a hard, fast fuck that lasted all night, but it was dark and we were insatiable. Tonight, I wanted to see him. All of him.

"Have at it." His words were confident, bordering on cocky with his arms spread wide over the back of the couch. I loved it right now, in the heat of passion, it was exactly what I needed.

I kicked off my shorts and dropped between his legs, letting my hands slide up his thighs until my fingertips were on his belt, his button, his zipper.

"Hips," I said and right away he lifted his hips to let me pull down his pants and I took advantage, taking them all the way off. Along with his boots. I feasted on the beauty that was Wheeler, even down to his long thick cock with the angry head, so hungry for what was coming next. "You are so fucking gorgeous," I told him honestly, feeling my pussy clench tight at the sight of him.

His grin kicked up lazily on one side at the compliment. "Too much talking, Doc." And there we were. Again. Back to the Doc bullshit.

"Annabelle," I insisted firmly, taking his thick cock in my hand and stroking in slow, sure moves. "My name is Annabelle. Say it." My gaze never left his even as my hand continued to work his cock, memorizing all the veins and the way they pulsed when he was turned on beyond comprehension.

Wheeler, stubborn bastard that he was, only grunted some incomprehensible sounds, and I squeezed his cock harder, stroking faster. "Fuck, Do—" His words were cut off abruptly.

"Say. My. Name."

"Annabelle," he bit out finally and I rewarded his obedience by leaning forward and swiping my tongue over the pearly bead of liquid at the very tip of his cock. "Oh fuck, Annabelle."

"Even better," I purred, enjoying having Wheeler at my mercy even if it was just for the moment. His cock was long but it was thick, making it a task to take him but I licked my lips with a smile and took him as far as I could, watching as he slowly came apart at the seams.

His hips bucked, and I knew I had him. I pressed, swallowing around the tip of his cock until they bucked again, nearly choking me.

"Fuck! Enough!" He grabbed my hair and tugged, which only sent more juices rushing between my thighs as I held my position, enjoying the way his cock pulsed in my mouth. His orgasm was imminent. "Come here."

I stood with a smile and hopped on his lap, freezing when he winced at the pain. "Shit." How could I have forgotten about his leg? His pain? That was the reason he was here, after all. "You can take it off."

"Not happenin'." His tone was firm, brooking no argument. At least not from a normal woman.

"Why not? I plan on doing all the work anyway." To punctuate my words I slid my slick pussy up and down his cock until he gripped my hips.

"Annabelle."

"Whatever," I growled, disappointed and angry but so damn horny that the only thing I cared about was sliding down his cock until he filled me all the way up. And that was just what I did. I used Wheeler like he was my very own fuck stick, bouncing on his big thick cock as if my pleasure was all that mattered. I rolled my hips, bounced against him and dug my nails into his flesh, all in the search for my next orgasm. "Fuck, yeah!"

His hands gripped my ass cheeks hard, and I didn't care. I loved that he couldn't control himself. When his hips started to thrust up into me and fireworks shot off behind my eyes, I fucked him harder. "Fuck. Shit. Don't stop."

LOADED

"Not. Gonna," I told him honestly, rolling my hips so his pelvic bone hit my clit and it was fucking incredible. My body tightened as the orgasm started at my toes, rising up like an erupting volcano just as Wheeler slipped one long finger between my cheeks and into my ass, knuckle deep and intensified my pleasure by a factor of a million. At least.

"Oh fuck! Shit! Fuck, Annabelle!" His orgasm came out powerful, Herculean as his hips bucked up into me, sending his come splashing against my convulsing walls while my body vibrated with need, pulsing around him like she wanted to eat him whole.

As soon as our breathing returned to normal, I slipped free of his body, of his touch and grabbed my clothes. "You're welcome to stay here tonight. Down here," I clarified before giving hm my back and walking away. My body still humming with pleasure.

Chapter Seven

Wheeler

Waking up in a dark room with no fucking clue where I was shouldn't have worried me as much as it did. But it had been a long damn time since it happened, and I was alarmed. But more than that, I wasn't coated in a thick layer of sweat and my pulse wasn't pounding while harsh breaths sawed out of me. Yanking the soft knit blanket off my body, I realized I was naked. Then I remembered.

Everything.

I remembered waking up to see a pair of big brown eyes, wide and worried in the dim light of the TV, looking deep into mine. Not only did I remember, but I knew I'd never forget the sight of Annabelle wrapping those lush pink lips around my cock or her riding my cock with wild, reckless abandon. Just thinking about it had my cock surging to life between my thighs. I smiled and pushed off the sofa, ignoring the twinge of pain in my leg and the phantom tingling that came when I slept in my prosthesis.

The good doctor was exactly the distraction I needed to push away the pain and the nightmares that wouldn't stop for any length of time no matter what I did or what I took. But Annabelle, she helped somehow, and though I didn't want to think on that too much, I did make my way up the narrow staircase where I found her in bed, covers kicked around her legs and falling half to the ground. Best of all? She was in nothing but a small scrap of plain black panties.

Without thinking I moved to the other side of the bed and slid between the sheets before gathering her in my arms. The soft, delicate skin of her back pressed to my chest and my cock nestled between her ass cheeks, tempting me beyond all fucking reason. Her soft, warm curves and that sensual flowery scent she wore combined with the smell of our sex lulled me into a twilight sleep that allowed unwanted images to creep in.

LOADED

The vast desert wasteland filled with nothing but rocks, hollowed out vehicles and dead animals.

Dead bodies lying on their backs, eyes open and stuck in that last moment of horror.

Friends, coughing and dying, praying and begging for their suffering to end. Hell. Pure, unadulterated fucking hell.

The images were too fucking much and my hands tightened, one on Annabelle's beautifully round breast and the other on the flare of her hips. I pinched her nipple and she squirmed against me, drawing my mind away from the images and to the way my cock sprang to life. A low, strangled moan escaped from her throat, waking her. Annabelle's head turned over her shoulder, hair mussed in the moonlight and a small frown marring the skin between her brows.

"Wheeler? What are you still doing here?" She tried to turn to face me and I held her in place.

"Shh," I whispered in her ear and pushed my hips forward. "You're why I'm still here. This is why."

She let out a little gasp of pleasure, and I smiled just before pressing my lips to that soft spot behind her ear, drawing out another, longer moan that had my cock hard enough it ached. When Annabelle arched into me, I grabbed her ass and spread her wide before sliding into her slick pussy, already clutching tight around me.

"Yes, Wheeler." Those two little words nearly tore apart my desire to delay her pleasure. Nearly, but the moans and cries made it impossible not to slow down so I could hear more of her erotic music. "Oh fuck, Wheeler. Yes, oh yes. Fuck me."

Hearing those words coming from her sweet, well-educated mouth made me fucking crazy.

One hand went to back to those beautiful tits, squeezing and kneading, pinching her nipples while she arched and squirmed under the force of her pleasure. One of her hands covered mine, encouraging me to apply more pressure.

"You want it hard? Rough?"

She nodded, breathless and panting though still moving her hips with every stroke of my cock.

"I can't hear you, Annabelle." The way her pussy tightened around my cock told me how much she liked it when I used her name, and just like that, I had another image of her sucking me off, and I surged deeper into the slick heaven of her cunt. "You want it hard?"

"Yes Wheeler. Fuck. Me. Harder."

At her words, I gave her exactly what she wanted. Hell, what we both wanted. While I kept up the steady pressure on her puckered nipples my other hand wrapped around her and gripped her throat, not enough to scare her but just enough to feel those little angel flutters deep inside of her. "Oh fuck, Annabelle. Such a tight little pussy."

"Yes," she moaned over and over, moving so every stroke brought me deeper and deeper inside of her. "More. Please."

That final, anguished plea tore apart any remnants of self-control I had remaining, or so I thought. When one delicate hand slid down her body and settled between her thighs to play with her clit, all traces of control vanished.

"Fuck!" I pumped into her hard and fast and wild, knowing we would both be sore as fuck tomorrow and not giving a damn, not when she felt so good. So tight and hot and wet, I could stay buried in her forever.

No, not forever, but a long goddamn time.

"More, Wheeler. Please." Her words were breathless and strangled and I felt my cock start to leak even as I pounded into her with everything I had, banishing any and every thought that tried to invade that wasn't centered on this woman. Her fingers danced around her clit, the light touch brushing against me with every stroke. That was all I needed.

My balls tightened and my spine started to tingle. I knew I wouldn't last much longer. "Annabelle, I need to feel that sweet pussy squeezing me tight."

LOADED

"Me. Too." She arched into me and my hand reluctantly left her tits and gripped her hip, holding her in place while I fucked away my demons and my pain, fucked her so hard and deep that I lost complete control the moment she did. Body glistening as her pussy convulsed violently around me, milking me and triggering my own orgasm that came fierce and powerful.

My body wasn't my own. For the first time in a long fucking time, I didn't give a damn. I tumbled down the mountain, burying my cock deep in her hungry body as my teeth sank into her soft flesh, hand squeezing her throat until she went limp even as little pulses continued to shake her body.

I froze for a moment, but Annabelle sucked in a breath and moaned before she let out a long, low groan. "Holy fuck. That was hot." Then she passed out for real, her even breathing telling me better than any words could, just how satisfied and spent she was.

I let myself stay and revel in the feel of her body still next to me for a long time, listening to her even breathing and watching the way the moon spilled into the room, highlighting a body I knew all too well. An hour, maybe more had passed and her scent was glued to my skin, stuck in my nose, and I felt my eyelids growing heavy.

Then I sat up, took one last look at Annabelle sleeping with a tiny smile curling her lips, and got the fuck out of there before I did something really stupid like fall asleep beside her. With my arms wrapped around her.

Chapter Eight

Annabelle

"You okay, Dr. Keyes?" Tish's concerned voice pulled me from an intense session of staring at my tablet until my vision blurred. Her dark brows dipped into a concerned vee and I knew then, I'd done a shit job of keeping my mind off everything but work.

"Yes, Tish, I'm good. Just distracted I guess." There was no guessing about it. Three days had passed since Wheeler made me feel so good that I slept an hour past my alarm and couldn't even find it in myself to give a damn. Three days where all I could do was think about those big blue eyes and that gorgeous face, the way he stared down at me as I took his dick in my mouth and made him growl my name. The way he'd come to me in the middle of the night and fucked me so dirty, so deliciously wicked that even now my nipples hardened at the thought of it.

"What's up, Tish?"

"Not much," she said, keeping her voice light even if she did a piss poor job of hiding her worry. "It's quiet for now. Why don't you go rest in your office for a few minutes? I'll page you when we need you."

Everything in me rebelled at the idea of going to rest while the nurses kept on working, but I was too distracted to be of any use to them now.

"Thanks, Tish. I'll be back in fifteen if you don't call," I told her, pointing a finger that made her laugh.

"All right, Dr. Keyes. I promise."

With a nod, I made my way down the hall to the shoebox office assigned to me by the hospital administrator. It wasn't meant to be comfortable because I didn't spend much time in here, completing most of my charting between patients or out at the nurse's station. The ER didn't slow down, not even in a small town like Opey, which served a dozen small towns in the area, most of them ranchers and cowboys. Staying out front helped keep me sharp and fresh, in the thick of the action.

LOADED

But now, in the quiet of my office I couldn't help but let my thoughts wander, again, to Wheeler. He hadn't been in yet for the painkillers, and he hadn't stopped by again in search of them. I wasn't foolish enough to believe that it meant his pain and nightmares were gone.

I knew for damn sure he hadn't confided in his brother about either issue. No matter how often I told myself that I shouldn't give a damn about him or his pain, I knew it was bullshit. Not because there was anything special about Wheeler, other than his almost beautiful features, but because I couldn't stand to see anyone hurting without wanting to help.

It was a curse but it was also a blessing that had allowed me to help thousands of people in my career. That was what I tried to remember when I thought of Wheeler, that I'd helped the people I could, those who wanted help instead of temporary relief.

A knock on the door pulled me from my thoughts, and I stood, wrapping my white coat around me with a smile. "That was fast, Tish." Fifteen minutes had gone by way too fast, and I was just about to tell her that when I opened the door, only it wasn't Tish.

"Can I help you?" My hand clutched the doorknob tight at the sight of the unfamiliar man with nondescript features.

"Uh, yeah, I hope so. Dr. Keyes, right?" He flashed a friendly smile, but the strain around the edges painted it as phony, I took in his features. He was tall, over six feet but not quite as tall as Wheeler, with short cropped brown hair and brown eyes even plainer than my own. He wore a black t-shirt underneath a fitted black zippered sweater, black jeans and scuffed black boots.

I didn't see private patients, hadn't since I returned to Texas. I could think of no reason he should be looking for me. All follow up patients were examined in the rooms, not the offices. Not to mention that I hadn't treated him. Ever. "Yes. What can I do for you?" I kept my tone firm but professional just in case the man was a patient, or the family member of a patient.

LOADED

"I'm looking for someone, and I'm hoping you can help me out."

That put me on edge even further. "I'm sorry, but we don't give out any information on our patients. There are laws to protect everyone's privacy."

He smiled again, but not before I caught the way his jaw clenched in annoyance. "My mistake. It's not a patient I'm looking for, at least I don't think she's a patient. She's an old friend of mine, Peaches Foster. Do you know her?"

My first instinct was to confirm that I knew her, but with all the unexplained injuries on Hardtail Ranch lately—bullet and knife wounds, bruised knuckles and the like—I hesitated. I didn't know what was going on over there, and I didn't ask, but now I wish I had. "I know Peaches." That was the only answer I was prepared to give him.

His smile rang fake again, and he leaned into my space, giving me a whiff of cigarette smoke.

"Great! You're just the person I'm looking for then. Peaches and I are old friends, thanks to some government work we did together a while back. She told me if I was ever in the area I should look her up." He smiled again and I waited for more information. "Stupid me, I thought a ranch would be easy to find, but it turns out this place is chock full of them."

The man had a smile that put me on edge and everything about his words rang false, making me wonder if he wasn't some disgruntled ex-lover. Peaches had only ever mentioned one person she considered a friend, Vivi who lived in Las Vegas.

"This is Texas, cowboy country," I said.

"Right," he said. From the tight line of his brows, I could tell he was impatient to get the answers he wanted, but he was willing to shoot the breeze to get it. A lot like the police officers and detectives I'd met while working in the ER.

"Can you give me directions to the ranch where she lives?"

LOADED

That wasn't happening, but I gave a friendly nod since I was alone with a strange man asking vague questions about my closest friend. "If you want to give me your information—"

Thankfully, an overhead page cut off my words. "Dr. Keyes to Trauma Room 4. Dr. Keyes, Trauma Room 4."

I nodded and flashed an apologetic smile that was as phony as his had been. "Sorry, but that's me. Gotta go." I wasn't sorry at all and the disbelieving look he gave me said as much.

"Wait, those directions?" He had an air of desperation about him now that I didn't like.

Tish paged me again, and I made a mental note to buy a bottle of her favorite perfume for the save.

"Leave your contact info with the front desk, and I'll make sure Peaches gets it, now really, I have to go." After grabbing my tablet and closing the door behind me, I skirted around the man and made my way to Trauma Room No. 4.

When I arrived, I found a six year old who'd lost a battle with a tractor and suddenly, I wished I was still back with the strange man who claimed to know Peaches. But I had to put him and Wheeler out of my mind and got busy trying to save the hand of the little boy.

Chapter Nine

Wheeler

"You look less like shit than you usually do." Holden's gruff words made me smile because he was a grouchy son of a bitch and that was as close to a compliment as he would ever get.

"Thanks Holden, you look pretty, too." The truth was I did feel good because that one night with Annabelle had given me nearly a full week of decent sleep. The first night I slept like a fucking baby, dreamlessly happy with the blank darkness of a deep sleep. Each night since the sleep came a little harder and lasted a shorter time than I wanted, but the nightmares stayed away and for that I was damn grateful.

"I'm glad to see you're doing better. Maybe now we can get some damn work done." His tone was gruff but none of us took it personally because that's just how Holden was, especially when it came to the ranching part of the MC operation. It was his baby, and he didn't tolerate any half-assing.

"I'm here and ready to work." I had plenty of energy and without the nightmares, I wasn't a total bastard. "Where are we going, anyway?"

He turned to me with a scowl that made me stand up straight. It was his worried scowl, not his run of the mill pissed off look. "To the back pasture. I picked up a downed calf on the security footage."

"Shit. Wolves again?" It was, I was learning, part of being a ranch owner.

"Don't know, but I guess we're about to find out." He killed the ignition on the Gator and we both lumbered out, making our way toward the sweet brown calf bawling her pain to the world. "Ah, fuck."

I felt exactly the same way looking at the animal writhing on the ground. "Hey girl, what's the matter?" She looked up at the sound of my voice and gave another 'moo' of distress while Holden crept around to check out the damage.

"Well?"

"Hind quarter is nearly split wide open. Definitely a fucking predator but at least it can be repaired."

A call to the vet and the calf would be fixed up good as new. "So there's a breach in the fence somewhere?"

Holden stood and nodded, staring off in the distance. "I checked the damn fence before breakfast. Twice and there's nothing I can see." His anger and frustration was palpable.

"What do you think it is and don't say *nothing* because I can hear it in your voice." I said. It was a good thing to know the other men so well, made it easier to trust them.

Holden sighed and turned to me. "I'm thinking that the fence was cut somewhere, on purpose, and that some lucky wolf strolled in at the most inopportune time for a late night snack. What I don't know is if it was a competing ranch or someone else." Arms crossed over his massive chest, Holden looked like a man with too much on his mind. I knew because it was an expression I'd worn often in the Army. Probably still did but I didn't spend much time in the mirror these days.

"Shit," I finally said, breaking the silence. "Who's gonna tell Gunnar?"

Holden's stoic expression transformed into a devious smile as he cut a look over at me. "You are, Vice Prez."

Dammit, he had me there. It was my responsibility, and since I accepted it and had done a damn good job as Gunnar's number two so far, it was up to me. But still, "Fucker."

Holden let out a loud belly laugh that I'd only witnessed twice in the years I'd known him. "Oh, I fuckin' plan to, as soon as we find the cut in the fence." It took two hours in the hot blazing sun before we found it, and we'd both missed it two times before. That's how good the intruder had been. "Could be a bolt cutter."

It could but the cuts were so fine and straight, cut with such precision that it was likely more advanced than what I'd get at the hardware store. "Maybe even a laser. Either way, human not animal." We spent fifteen minutes mending the fence and made our way, slowly and damned reluctantly, back to the main house.

To Gunnar.

"Ready for this?" Holden killed the engine and turned to me, a serious expression on his face.

"Fuck no, but this is part of being a Bastard, right?" I snorted. "Wouldn't say no to a beer though."

Holden laughed. "Amen, brother."

We found Gunnar on the back porch with Peaches on his lap, the two of them making out like horny teenagers. If I had a dollar for every time I caught those two going at it, I could leave the ranch, the MC, and the club behind and live my life on an island somewhere, doing whatever people did who knew how to relax and enjoy life. "Get a room," I said when we were close enough to startle them.

Peaches froze and slowly turned with a mischievous smile on her face. "Hey guys, what's up?" At the expression on my face or Holden's her grin dimmed and she was on her feet. "Seriously. What's up?"

I appreciated that about Peaches, that she didn't pretend MC business wasn't serious as fuck. She was always willing to help however she could. Hell, she was more of a badass than most men I knew and served with.

I sucked in a breath and held Gunnar's gaze while I told them about the calf and the fence. "It was definitely precision work, nothing sloppy at all. And we weren't meant to find it."

"I'll check the security footage," Peaches said, bare feet already on the move into the house.

When she was gone, Gunnar let out a string of curses. "Farnsworth. Has to be." His fist landed on the wooden railing with a crack that could have been the wood or his hand. "Goddammit, this shit is never ending!"

LOADED

He was right about that. It turns out that being in a MC was a lot like being in the Army. Enemies were everywhere and just when you defeated one, another motherfucker was right around the corner.

"Hell, yeah. I bet it's him," I agreed. It was the only thing that made sense. "Has Peaches said anything to you?"

"You think she's keepin' secrets?" His glare and the way his hands balled into angry fists said he was spoiling for a fight.

Not today. "Calm the fuck down, man. I'm asking if he's reached out, left messages or any shit like that. Anything to say he's close by." If she was my girl, I'd be pissed too and ready to take on the world. That's why he had me to keep his ass in line.

"No." His shoulders fell, and I knew the silence was more bothersome than the cut fence. "Not a goddamn thing."

"So what are we gonna do?" It was the first time Holden had spoken, his deep voice and southern twang bringing it back to what was important.

"Protect Peaches." Gunnar and I said at the same time, making Holden grin.

"Protect Peaches from what?" sounded from behind me.

"Damn woman, you move around like a fucking ninja."

Peaches had reappeared silently, not even the squeaky ass door made a sound, which meant she'd been eavesdropping. "Didn't you hear?"

"Not everything," she said with a saucy grin. "That's why I'm asking." Armed with her sturdy black laptop, she looked fierce and ready to do battle.

Gunnar grabbed her by the arm before she could sit down. He tugged her to the other end of the porch that wrapped three quarters around the house, but not far enough away that we couldn't read their body language. Or hear the harshly spoken whispers neither of them did a damn thing to hide. Gunnar told her he put her under increased protection whether she wanted it or not, and Peaches with her scowl and the way she clutched the laptop, had threatened him with either bodily harm or a lack of sex. Or both. Finally, she stepped back and shook her head.

"Stubborn ass men," she growled and marched back to Holden and me without giving us a glance. She dropped down in the chair she'd just shared with Gunnar and flipped open her laptop.

"I'm not some goddamned princess in a tower. In case you've forgotten, I wired this whole damn place with top of the line electronic surveillance."

Her fingers flew over the keyboard, and I watched, as I always did, in awe of her skills.

"Motherfucker! Look." She pointed at the screen, and we all crowded around her.

I looked at the black screen but only saw the moving time counter. "I don't see anything," I said.

"Exactly. And it's just for twelve minutes. This black screen means they didn't just cut the wires. See?" She fast forwarded the video and sure enough, twelve minutes later the picture returned and the clock kept spinning.

Gunnar started at the video and said, "What the fuck could he possibly have done in twelve minutes? He couldn't even get to the main house on foot in that time." Gunnar wasn't looking for an answer, he was scared for Peaches.

But problem-solving was what I did best. "Recon," I told him easily, ignoring the glare he sent my way because he didn't want a fucking answer. Too damn bad. "It's what I'd do. Come in and get a layout of the land so I'd be prepared when I came back. The problem is, we don't know what he's planning."

Did he want to kill Peaches or all of the Reckless Bastards? Did she have something he wanted? "Whatever it is, we need to be prepared."

Gunnar added, "You're right. We need to come up with a schedule so there are eyes on Peaches at all times."

"Gunnar, babe, please." Peaches stood and shoved the laptop at Holden who took it cautiously, like he thought the damn thing might bite him. "We can't have the guys exhausted and unfocused. Farnsworth, if this was him, won't strike with a lot of people around unless he absolutely has to. Fewer loose ends to tie up that way."

"We'll talk about this later," Gunnar told her firmly, as if that would do anything to quiet the woman.

"We can talk about it now."

I was just about to tell them that was a fight for another time, when the sound of Maisie's laughter grew closer. The little girl had the uncanny ability to calm even the most shit-tastic of situations.

"Look who I found!" she said in high-pitched voice, full of joy when she came into view. She was holding on to Annabelle like they were best friends, laughing and smiling brightly.

"What are you doing here?" I asked her. The growl and the dick-ish tone weren't necessary, but I wasn't prepared to see her just yet. Not after...*everything*.

Annabelle frowned, looking pretty as fuck in black slacks and a silky red blouse that did an excellent job of hiding the differences between us, and then turned her gaze to Peaches, effectively dismissing me. "Can we talk for a minute?"

"Sure, what's up?" Peaches leaned forward expectantly, but Annabelle's gaze swung from Peaches to Gunnar and back.

"Maybe we should do this in private?"

Peaches grinned at her. "There's so much shi-stuff going on around here that I'll probably have to tell them. Tell me here and this way I won't have to." She smiled at Maisie and nodded towards the back door. "Go on in and see if Martha has a snack for you."

"Yay, I hope she made cookies!" Gunnar's little sister scrambled out of Annabelle's arms and ran inside, letting the screen door smack shut behind her.

All eyes swung to Annabelle and she shoved her hands into the pockets of her expensive slacks, which fell around a pair of hot pink sneakers. Odd. "I've been thinking about this for a couple of days now, and I wasn't sure if I should say anything or not. I mean, I figured if you wanted me to know you would have told me, and I didn't want to butt in—"

"Annabelle," Peaches said with a calm voice. "You're babbling."

"Right," she said as her cheeks pinkened adorably. "A man came to the hospital looking for you the other day and something about it didn't feel right."

"What? Didn't?" I barked at her. "Are you in trouble?" She wasn't my problem and she sure as shit wasn't an MC problem, but I knew Gunnar wouldn't see it that way because Peaches wouldn't.

I earned another glare, but she didn't say one fuckin' word to me. She turned back to Peaches. "He said you were old friends, and I wasn't sure if that meant old lovers, but I remembered that you only ever talk about Vivi. He wanted directions to the ranch, and luckily I was called away before I could give them to him." She took a deep breath, wringing her hands nervously. "It hasn't set right with me since, so I decided to come out here and tell you, so you could decide how to deal with it."

Peaches took in Annabelle's words slowly, carefully logging every detail into the database she called a brain. "What did he look like?"

"Nothing out of the ordinary. Decent looking but not stand out handsome with short brown hair and plain brown eyes. No blemishes, birth marks or other distinguishing features." Her shoulders fell. "Sorry. The best way to describe him is, well, nondescript."

"Sounds like cop speak," I said out of the blue and completely unnecessary based on the glares Holden and Gunnar sent my way.

Annabelle glared too. "I can call the cops and give them this information if you prefer?" She folded her arms, daring me to say something else to piss her off.

Peaches held up a hand to stop us both. "Shit. It's definitely him," Peaches said with a groan. "Did he leave a name?"

"No. I told him if he gave me his info I'd pass it on and that just seemed to piss him off."

"You did the right thing, Annabelle. Thanks." Peaches grabbed her laptop from Holden and sighed. "Let's go inside and have a chat while these stubborn bastards talk about me behind my back." She winked at Gunnar, blew him a kiss and walked inside.

As soon as they were out of earshot, Gunnar spoke. "Get the guys and tell them to meet in the bunkhouse ASAP."

Chapter Ten

Annabelle

"So you used to be a spy?" My head was spinning so much that two drinks ago, Peaches had started adding a splash of bourbon to my lemonade. But a splash wasn't enough. Not with the crazy story she'd been telling me for the past hour.

"Not a spy, no. Not even officially an employee of the government. Just a consultant. That's the fancy word they use for freelancers."

"But that's not how you got started working for the government?"

"No, they caught me as a kid hacking into some places I shouldn't, and you know the deal. They used my skills while I worked off my punishment without a record." She said it so casually I shook my head, but *no*, I didn't know the deal.

"Are you freaking out?" she asked.

I was, a little bit. "You've led an exciting life, Peaches. How could I not know any of this? I mean, I've always wondered how you're able to wear fabulous shoes and your gadget collection puts everyone else to shame." I was ashamed to admit that I assumed Gunnar paid for it all.

She sighed and sipped her own, bourbon-less lemonade, taking her time to work through whatever was bothering her. "I never planned to tell you any of this."

That stung a little, and I guess it must've shown on my face because Peaches looked guilty as hell. "It's fine. We're all entitled to our secrets."

She arched a brow. "Like the terrible job you and Wheeler are doing of pretending like you hate each other?"

I felt my cheeks heat even though I wasn't ashamed that Wheeler and I were using each other for sex. It was damn good sex from a man who was ten thousand percent sex on a stick, and as untouchable as the sun. "It's not pretending, but yes we have been sleeping together. On and off. Mostly off."

Her copper brows furrowed, making her look just as confused as I felt. It didn't make sense, his attitude and clear mistrust. I hadn't done a damn thing to earn either.

"What's his problem, then?"

I shrugged. "Who knows? Maybe he hates that he wants a prissy bitch like me."

Peaches barked out a laugh that startled me for a moment. "You do have your prissy moments but it's more like they slip out once in a while. It's all part of your charm."

That was nice of her to say, but I knew the truth. "I'm a snob." I couldn't tell her about the pills I was no longer prescribing or giving to him. It wouldn't be good for me or Wheeler for her to know that. "Aren't there more important things to talk about than a temperamental biker?"

Peaches' bright red lips snapped shut at my quick subject change. She arched her brows and flashed an impressed smile. "I never planned to tell you any of this because I hoped you'd never need to know. I'm not ashamed of my work, but most of it is secret and most people can't resist asking questions. The less you know, the better."

I understood that. There were a lot of secrets on Hardtail Ranch. "Like all the questions I haven't asked about all the off the books medical help the guys need?"

"Wheeler hasn't told you about the Reckless Bastards?" The surprise in her voice must've shown on my face because she rolled her eyes as a low frustrated growl tore through the quiet kitchen.

"We don't have that kind of relationship. He drops by whenever he feels like it and he always leaves me satisfied so I always let him in. We fuck like wild animals, and he leaves. The end."

"Right. I'm surprised you put up with that."

"It's a cheap fuck, no strings attached. It works for me for now. It's not like I have the time or the inclination to date anyone right now, but I do love sex with that man." It was my turn to arch my brow at her attempt to change the subject. Again.

"Anyway, they're a motorcycle club and sometimes that brings a different set of troubles."

"Is that another name for a biker gang?"

"They aren't a gang. They are an official club whose members share common interests. They are also military veterans and business partners. Brothers. When trouble comes for one of them, one of *us*," she corrected with a wistful smile, "it comes for all of us. Me included."

"Okay so you're one big happy family. Why can't I know any of that?" It just didn't make any sense. "I thought we were friends." I heard the hurt in my voice, and I wasn't ashamed of it, because I thought this friendship was different.

"We are, and that's exactly why I wanted you to be ignorant of everything that was going on here. Not that I even really know half of what's actually going on most of the time, but I figured the less you knew the better. And honestly, the whole Farnsworth stuff is kind of a recurring nightmare."

I listened as Peaches told me all about the mysterious job in Europe, nothing specific, that had gone wrong. The sudden and even more mysterious deaths of her co-workers in said job, and the man—or men—currently coming after her. Farnsworth. It was a lot to take in all at once and process. It was all so far removed from my life. Hell from anything I'd ever experienced, first or second hand, in my life. My legs shook as I walked toward the cabinet that passed for a bar in the main house, pulling out the bourbon and pouring it over the ice and the splash of lemonade already in the glass. "So this guy really is a spy or some kind of undercover operative?"

I was sure I sounded like an idiot.

Peaches drained her glass and said, "The most undercover of the undercovers. I've worked with a few different Farnsworths in my career."

"You say it all so casually, and yet I can't seem to wrap my mind around any of it." But I was good at the details. "You still don't know what he wants?"

"Probably to kill me," she said in such a monotone voice that I froze, drink halfway to my mouth.

"Peaches, stop."

"You deal with life and death every day, Annabelle."

"And that's exactly why I don't take either lightly."

"Good. Because this is the other reason I didn't want to tell you any of this. It's the reason I'm sorry I kept it from you. Farnsworth has already, somehow, made the connection, between either me and you, or you and the club."

I heard what she was saying, but all I could focus on was what she *wasn't* saying.

"I'm in danger?"

Peaches gave one sharp nod, guilt swimming in her eyes. "Yep. And it doesn't matter what you know or don't know. I know that now, and I'm sorry, Annabelle."

I wanted to be upset, to yell and scream at both Peaches and Wheeler for keeping me in the dark when they knew exactly how much danger was lurking around them. But getting upset wouldn't change anything, so I nodded. "Does any of this have to do with your mysterious trip to New York?"

She nodded. "It all does. That's where I lived when, well when this all first started to go wrong. There's been a lot of lying low and all that, but yeah. We went back to see if we could figure out why Farnsworth is after me."

Her gaze slid to the side like she was hiding something. At this point I didn't know if I even wanted to know what it was. But I felt compelled.

"You don't know?" I asked her, incredulously.

She shook her head, her expression mystified as copper curls came to a rest on her shoulders. "I can't say for sure. The op didn't go as planned, but they don't sometimes. If there's something else happening, I don't know what it is. That pisses me off and terrifies me." Peaches shrugged and twirled a lock of hair around her finger. "Everything was mostly scrubbed clean so it wasn't helpful."

I heard what she wasn't saying. "You found something that you're not sure about, and you don't want to tell anyone." It wasn't a question. Now that I had a much clearer picture of her life, I could see the signs.

She nodded. "It's not just that I don't want to, I can't. If I do, everything I've done will have been for nothing."

I didn't know what to say to that. It all seemed so implausible but Peaches seemed to believe it. All of it, including the danger I was in, so I said the only thing I could.

"Apology accepted."

"Good. Because I think you need to move to the ranch until Farnsworth has been dealt with."

That was not happening. "I can't do that, Peaches. I like having my space. I *need* my space." Not to mention the fact that Wheeler would probably shit a brick if I stayed here.

"I'll be fine."

"You won't. That's what I need you to understand. Farnsworth will kill you just to get back at us, to throw us off balance." She was fired up, and I knew Peaches sincerely believed it all, because I believed her.

"So what, I'm supposed to live in your guestroom, driving an extra fifteen miles back and forth to the hospital for an indefinite amount of time?" That sounded completely unreasonable, though not when the alternative was death.

"I didn't want to have to do this, Annabelle, but you've left me no choice."

A small smile crossed my face at her theatrics. I sat back against the wall and waited.

"No choice?"

She folded her arms over her big boobs and pursed her lips before she spoke. "I need an extra set of eyes on Maisie at all times. Between me and you and Martha, we should have it handled. At all times."

Suddenly, I knew what she meant. "Low blow, Peaches." Bringing that adorable little girl into it, knowing I wouldn't be able to deny her that, was unfair. And it worked like a charm.

She shrugged, completely unapologetic. "You left me with no other option. I'll get the empty master suite at the other end of the hall ready for you. It'll be your own little space." Gratitude and hope swam in her eyes, but more than anything I saw relief.

"Thanks, Annabelle, and I really am sorry."

"I'm only sorry you didn't think you could trust me with your secrets."

"Again? Wheeler ringing any bells?"

I shrugged. "There's nothing to tell, but I'm happy to provide details if you want."

"Later," she said, flashing a wide smile. "Whenever their meeting is over, one of the guys will take you to get some of your things. Until then, how about a proper bourbon?"

She read my mind, and I smiled, lifting my glass up for a refill. Sometimes a girl just needed a little bit of liquid courage to get through the really tough shit.

Chapter Eleven

Wheeler

"Try not to take too long, Doc." I didn't have to growl at her the way I did, but I could have slapped Gunnar for telling me to keep an eye on Annabelle while she prepared to stay on the ranch until shit blew over. I insisted on driving my own truck, and she sat beside me, quiet and pensive. Probably trying to figure out how the hell she got sucked into this mess.

"It'll take as long as it takes for me to hand wrap my good China." She snorted and pushed open the door before I even killed the engine, giving me a quick eyeroll then walking up the steps into her house.

I followed her inside and grabbed her shoulder. "Just a sec." Now that we knew it was Farnsworth, we had to assume no place was safe. "Stay here." Instead of waiting for her to argue with me, I went inside, checking all the rooms on both floors until I was satisfied the place was safe. "Come on in, Doc." I called out.

When I got back downstairs, Annabelle had kicked off her shoes and grabbed a beer while she surveyed the contents of her fridge. "Help yourself to a beer and the television. It'll take me about an hour." She picked up her bottle and disappeared up the stairs, leaving me alone in her space.

Her place always surprised me. It was more colorful than I imagined her place would be. Splashes of yellow and red, bright purple and emerald green dotted the otherwise black and white furniture. She seemed so prissy everywhere except the bedroom, I half expected her place to be pink and beige. But it wasn't. This was her space, where she let her true self shine, and it was her to a tee.

Goddammit, the last thing I wanted was to understand her. She was about to stay on the ranch. Under MC protection, which meant I couldn't keep getting mixed up with her. Not while she slept under Gunnar's roof. Hell, I wanted her so bad I'd argued against having her stay on the ranch, insisting she didn't need our help.

I felt like a real asshole when Gunnar pointed out that Farnsworth already knew where she worked. If he knew where she lived, he probably knew about my semi-regular visits. Which meant she needed our help.

And now she had it, which meant I couldn't have her.

Maybe not once we were on the ranch, but we weren't there now, were we?

Fuck no, we weren't. Five seconds later I climbed the stairs and found her bent over inside her closet, heart-shaped ass encased in denim. Teasing me the way it wiggled.

"Need some help, Doc?"

She froze at the sound of my voice and looked over her shoulder, sending a bolt of dark arousal through me as I imagined her naked, letting me fuck her hard from behind.

"No thanks, I got it." She turned back, dismissing me.

Too bad my cock was already awake and stirring. I needed her, bad, and I had to have her.

I leaned over and purred in her ear. "Are you sure?" I rubbed my hands over the globe of her ass, up and down her thighs, letting my thumbs graze the almost invisible seam between her legs. "Because I'm right here."

I knew I had her when she tossed her head back and let out a sensual moan that had my cock standing up and taking notice. "What do you want, Wheeler?"

"I want to fuck you, Annabelle. It's been too long since I felt you fall apart around my cock." She moaned again and wiggled her ass against my cock.

"Fuck me, then." That was it, easy acceptance of what we both wanted. It was a part of what made her so damn appealing. So fucking irresistible.

"I will," I promised, pulling her toward me and slowly stripping her out of her slacks and silky blouse.

LOADED

Her doctor's clothes. She was fucking perfect, thin and feminine, with a narrow waist and hips a little bigger than they needed to be and her tits, were slightly more than a handful. But the way some of her pussy hairs were already slick? That had my mouth watering, knowing she wanted me just as fucking bad.

"But first," I told her and leaned forward, inhaling the musky scent of her wet, turned on pussy.

"Yes?"

"First I want you to show me the dirty girl I know you can be." Before I could say another word, her hands were on my body, pulling off my clothes before I stilled them.

"What do you want me to do to you, Annabelle?"

With a coy smile, she bit down on her bottom lip and gave me a long look. "Lie down. On the floor."

I didn't know whether to be insulted or turned on, but the scent of her desire swirled in the air and my cock was rock hard from just looking at her. So I got down until her soft plush carpet was against my back. "Now what?"

"Now," she laughed and kissed her way up my body, licking a trail of heat from my balls to the tip of my cock. "You're totally at my mercy." She settled her knees on either side of my head and all I needed to do was flick my tongue out and the taste of her pussy slid down my throat. "Yes!"

I closed my eyes and tasted her, every drop as it slid onto my tongue and down my throat, coating my lips and chin as she ground against me, taking her pleasure. My tongue slipped inside her pussy and her thighs tightened enough to make my vision turn dark around the edges.

"Oh fuck, Wheeler! Yes!" She bent forward until our gazes connected and reached down to grab a handful of my hair, grinding intensely and allowing me to see exactly what she was feeling. "Yes," she moaned again, sliding back and forth until my face was coated with her juices and my cock leaked onto my belly.

Her orgasm was close, I could tell by the way her thigh muscles trembled and how her nails dug into my scalp as she tried to grab anything to keep her grounded as pleasure lifted her high in the air.

"Uh-huh," I grunted when she tried to lift off as the pleasure overwhelmed her, gripping her ass to hold her in place while I licked and sucked her beyond the point of pleasure. To the point where her cries turned agonizing and almost painful as her body vibrated with satisfaction. To the point where laughter bubbled out of her between convulsions.

"Wheeler! God, yes! Oh yes!" She shook and fell forward before rolling to her side, heaving in several lungsful of air. "I need a moment to recover," she panted. "But in the meantime," she let her words trail off with a distracted grin as she kissed her way down my body, paying extra special attention to my cock.

"Don't tease me."

"I wouldn't dream of it," she said, wrapping a hand around my cock. "How do you like your cock sucked, Wheeler?" Her eyes were as playful as her tone, even the way she gripped me like an oversized lollipop, dipping her tongue into the slit on my cock head.

"That's a damn good start," I somehow managed on a groan, doing my best to keep from thrusting deep into that hot wet mouth. "Again." Heat flared in her eyes at the command and she obeyed. "Again," I growled and again she obeyed, making my cock throb.

In the next moment her full lips were wrapped around the tip of my cock, her dark gaze holding mine like a magnet as the O of her mouth slid down my cock until I hit the back of her throat. She moaned like she was enjoying this as much as I was, which wasn't fucking possible.

"You like that?" Her question came out breathless and proud, and then she went back to work before waiting for my answer.

But I wasn't fooled. Women these days loved to pretend they liked it rough, that a rough throat pounding turned them on as much as it did men. But when push came to shove, they never meant it. Not really. I flexed my hips up and slid my cock down her throat, a perfect way to test her commitment. "Yeah."

Her big brown eyes started to water. I waited for her to pull back, but she didn't. Instead she swallowed around my cock, and I went temporarily blind.

"Oh fuck," I breathed. I looked down at her with a smile. Challenge accepted, babe.

I sat up, resting one hand behind me and the other sifted through her hair until I had a good handful, holding her right where I wanted her as I slid my cock in and out of her mouth, deeper with every stroke. In an act of trust that nearly had me blowing my load, Annabelle put her hands behind her back, trusting me to make myself feel good without actually hurting her. She moaned and the vibration made my blood pulse.

"Mmm, mmm."

My hips moved faster and faster as my cock disappeared down her throat, the slick sound of skin on skin making me harder as Annabelle swallowed. Again.

"Fuck me!" I bellowed.

She laughed and sucked which made my eyes cross, but when one hand fell from her back and landed between her legs and she let out that low moan, I lost my shit and tore my cock out of her mouth.

"Fuck me, AB. I can't wait to fuck your mouth again but right now I need to see how wet you got from sucking my cock." I pulled her up the length of my body and rolled on top of her, flexing my hips so my cock rammed her clit over and over.

"See for yourself," she said on a sultry moan, rubbing two fingers across my lips so I could taste the musky sweetness of her pussy. "So, so wet."

Ah, fuck it, I loved it when she turned into a dirty little slut. Licking my lips with a groan, the head of my cock slipped into her opening, and fuck me, she was drenched and the scent of sex permeated the room.

We fucked each other, hard and fast, frantic and almost out of control as we both chased our pleasure like they were our demons. I pounded hard and fast, and she arched into me, offering her sweet tits while I fucked her until my spine felt like it might crack apart.

"Wheeler," she moaned as she squirmed against me, digging her heels into my ass and clinging to my shoulders. "Oh, fuck, yes, Wheeler!"

I gripped her tight, holding her still while I pounded hard and fast until her orgasm hit, pulsing around me in violent flutters, bringing me even closer to the edge. Then her pussy began to pulse in a steady stream as another orgasm hit, the friction of her slick pussy combined with her sweet cries, gave me a small shove so I teetered on the edge. And finally, a rush of liquid so loud and furious and sexy as hell, my own orgasm finally pushed us off the ledge together, tumbling in a haze of colors and cries of pleasure. "Oh, AB, fuck!"

She continued to shiver and convulse even when I collapsed on top of her, her tight cunt still pulsing around my cock, sucking me dry.

I barely rolled off of her before I passed out.

Chapter Twelve

Annabelle

When I woke up, it wasn't morning yet, not even close judging by how bright the moon was shining. My body hummed with pleasure and a lazy, satisfied grin crossed my face as I thought about how wild and sexy Wheeler had made me feel. How desired. How naughty I felt. It was the best sex of my life and surprisingly, Wheeler hadn't bailed in the middle of the night.

Behind me he slept soundly, his breathing even and deep with one arm draped over my waist. The nightmares seemed to be in hiding for the night, so I slid from his grasp, grabbed my robe and headed out of the bedroom, letting him soak up a few more hours of peaceful sleep.

I scanned the living room and then the kitchen before grabbing a couple boxes from my utility closet, which I filled with supplies because I knew that whatever was happening, the Reckless Bastards would need my medical services. I packed gauze, antiseptic, needles, staples and anything else I might've needed to dress non-fatal wounds. When the boxes were full to my satisfaction, I shut them and stacked them beside the front door.

Next, I went to my fridge and pulled out everything that could go bad, packing what I figured could be eaten and tossing leftovers that were probably already beyond their expiration date. Staying at the ranch wasn't an ideal situation, but I made a promise to Peaches, so I pushed the doubts out of my mind and kept on moving, stopping only when the sound of Wheeler's phone buzzing became too frequent to ignore.

I wasn't trying to butt into his business. I knew, as I crept over to his phone and jacket draped over the arm of the sofa, it could be anyone calling him this time of night. Including or maybe especially a woman in search of the good time he just gave me. I ignored the relief I felt at seeing Gunnar's name and turned on my heels, heading right towards the big sexy man sleeping on my bedroom floor.

He was on his back, the sheet resting dangerously low on his hips, just low enough that I could see those muscles that turned even the smartest girl's brain to mush. The path of dark hair disappeared beneath the bulge in the sheet, a hint of the gleaming metal from the bottom of his leg.

"Wheeler," I whispered, keeping a few feet of distance between us at first. "Wheeler," I called out to him a little louder this time, giving his shoulders a gentle shake. "Gunnar is calling you." I held out his phone to him.

His blue eyes snapped open, and he jackknifed into a sitting position in one second and had my body pinned beneath him in the next. He blinked and his eyes seemed focused as he stared down at me until I began to squirm.

"Wheeler it's me, Annabelle. Dr. Keyes."

"I know that, goddammit. Don't *ever* wake me up like that. Got it?" His voice came out on a low, angry growl, and I nodded quickly, trying like hell to ignore the way his half erection pressed right between my thighs, adding delicious friction to my clit. Wheeler grunted when his cock landed on damp flesh, and I arched into him, silently begging for more. "Tease."

"Sorry." I apologized instantly, remembering the real reason I was in here. "Gunnar's been blowing up your phone."

It was just the distraction he and I both needed because it felt a little too intimate to wake up together, ready to fuck again so soon. He grabbed his phone and turned away, which gave me the perfect opportunity to start packing some clothes and toiletries, enough to last a week at least. I hoped to be back in my own bed by this time next week, so I moved quickly, before Wheeler turned back into the asshole version of himself.

"Right, I'll be there," he growled angrily into the phone. "I said I'll fuckin' be there, didn't I?" His footsteps sounded behind me. "We gotta go. Some shit's gone down at the club."

I nodded, more than halfway finished packing. "There are boxes beside the door that need to go in your truck. If you get started on those, I'll be finished in just a few minutes." He looked like he wanted to argue, but still he hadn't told me one damn thing about was going on or the danger it posed to me, so I ignored his stares until he walked away.

When he returned I was giving the place one final glance.

"Ready?" he asked.

"Yep." I handed him two bags of trash and grabbed my suitcase before pulling the door shut and locking it. I felt like someone was watching, but maybe I was being paranoid. Maybe knowing about the trouble simply made me more aware of it. Or *too* aware of it.

We rode in total silence, not even the radio played until we turned under the Hardtail Ranch sign, and he said, "While you're staying at the main house, we should keep our distance."

I snorted a laugh that was half bitter and half amused before sliding him a glance.

"Afraid people might find out you actually like me? Don't worry Wheeler, I'm sure I'll find some way to survive without your cock. I mean I *did* manage to do it for decades of my life, not to mention those quiet periods when you don't find me useful."

"Dammit, it's not like that, Annabelle." He seemed offended, but I wasn't buying it. I knew Wheeler's game because, like all addicts, he thought his problems and his pain were unique to him, somehow different or worse than everyone else's.

"Thanks for your help tonight, Wheeler." I didn't need one of his phony apologies, and I was getting sick as hell of his attitude after we had sex, like I'd somehow tricked him into doing something he didn't want to, which was total bullshit.

LOADED

The car finally came to a stop right in front of the main house, gleaming now in the moonlight. He turned off the engine and spoke into the silence. "Listen, Annabelle."

Not interested in that shit. I pushed open the door and jumped out before he could say another word, tossing the last ten pain pills he would get from me on the passenger seat.

"Take care of yourself Wheeler."

I grabbed my backpack, a suitcase and a box, knowing the rest of my belongings would make it inside by morning.

As hard as it was, I didn't look back at Wheeler once. Not until I was sure he'd gone to deal with whatever happened at their club. Then I went up to my temporary room and slowly mentally unpacked everything I'd learned in the past twelve hours while I literally unpacked my bags.

Chapter Thirteen

Wheeler

"What the fuck happened?" After dropping the doc off at the main house, I gunned it across the property to The Barn Door, stopping only to get some backup ammo. Just in case it was needed. I found Ford slumped in the seat he rarely used because the damn kid was like a jacked up rabbit, excited, eager and deadly. But not now. The blood dripping from his head gave me some clue. "Well?"

To his credit, the prospect tried to stand up because he was fresh from service and hadn't lost the rigidity drilled into us from day one. But whatever had cracked him in the head, probably gave him a concussion, and he fell back in the chair.

"Three masked gunmen. One cracked me in the head with the butt of his gun before I could tell them to get the fuck out. I blacked out instantly. Woke up to the sound of gunfire."

"Shit. Any casualties?" I braced myself for the answer, knowing that no matter what the answer was, I couldn't lose my shit.

"No."

I sucked in a deep breath, determined to stay calm as the words sank in. "What?"

Ford's mouth twisted into something like a grin and his massive shoulders rose and fell in a shrug. "I know, weird as fuck right? I'm happy about it but the Prez ain't."

And that was just the reminder I needed to get my feet moving. "Make sure you get that head checked out before you even think of going to sleep, Prospect."

"I will," he grumbled behind me, but I was already moving inside the club, scanning the room in search of the familiar faces of the Reckless Bastards. It wasn't hard with all the overhead lights on, which on its own wasn't weird.

But to have so many people milling about in their sexy, kinky attire with the energy efficient lights burning bright overhead was...strange as fuck. It was unsettling, like somebody had invaded this space and made it feel unsafe.

"Goddamn fuckers." A quick look at the main bar to my right, and I spotted Saint frowning up at his girlfriend, Hazel, who was wrapping his arm. "What the fuck happened to you?"

Saint's gaze reluctantly left Hazel's face. "Flying glass. I'm fine, Hazel is just being fussy." The smile on his lips said he didn't mind one bit. "I'm letting her because it's her first shoot out."

"Asshole," she muttered, smacking the bandage on his arm a little harder than she needed to. "We're fine up here. Everyone's a little shaken up so we've got shots of the good whiskey going around."

I nodded and kept moving through the crowd until I spotted Gunnar in the corner with the mayor of Opey. He caught my gaze and nodded toward the now empty dance cages that were usually suspended in the air. I made my way over, spotting Cruz along the way.

"Three gunmen and no casualties?" That didn't sit right with me. I was grateful but shit like this happened by design.

Cruz shrugged. "They weren't even trying to hit anyone, shooting up in the air like a bunch Nineties' gangsters. Dumb fucks." He shook his head and looked around the room at the club goers comforting each other. "I'm glad no one got hurt. There's a lot of Texas society in here tonight."

I shrugged, taking his word for it. I made a promise to Gunnar as his number two, but I left the politicking to the rest of the MC. "Do you know who?"

"Goddamn Diablos, that's who." Gunnar's abrupt arrival and gruff words were no surprise. He loved this place and was determined to keep it safe. And clean. "It makes no fucking sense either. I remember those fucks, Beto and Juno is the small one, the leader. We scared them off, for good, I was sure and this shit," he waved at the bullet holes dotting the ceiling and walls, "doesn't make any fucking sense."

LOADED

I looked closer at the walls, inspecting the holes that splashed in an arch. "Automatic weapons? They used automatic weapons and nobody got hurt." This shit just got stranger and stranger. "Did they say anything?" Gangsters like the Diablos couldn't help but brag. It was part of how they were built.

"Nothing helpful. That's why we were so eager to get a hold of you. Took a while," he said, part pissed off and part fishing expedition.

I shrugged. "You know how women are when it comes to packing." Hell I didn't know what it meant, and it wasn't true anyway, Annabelle had packed her shit the way she did everything, efficiently.

Gunnar's response was just a grunt. "I figured your particular skill set might produce better results than just beating the fuck out of them, as fun as that might be." How he managed in a smile in the middle of this shit show, I had no clue.

"How pissed is the mayor?"

Surprise flickered in Gunnar's eyes, which made Cruz snort beside me until I sent my elbow into his side. "Offered up the help of Opey PD if we choose to turn them in when we're done with 'em. His words."

"I guess they really do things different down in Texas." I enjoyed the smile for as long as it lasted, knowing that in a few moments I'd have to slide my game face on the way I always did before an interrogation. "Where are they?"

"The black shed. Ford's buddy Romeo is keeping an eye out."

"That fucker with the neck tattoo?" I wasn't judging but he seemed an odd choice.

"Yep. Former MP."

"Prospect material?"

Gunnar shrugged. "We'll see."

I gave a short nod, happy we were all caught up on that. "I'll let you know what I find."

LOADED

This part of the MC was no different from the Army, sliding every piece of me into different boxes so that only the basest, most primal part of me was left. The part that was good at his job. For me it was sharpshooting, languages and interrogation, and the part that would do anything to get a result.

"I'm coming with you," Cruz said, jumping in the passenger seat a moment before I took off. "Maybe I'll pick up some skills."

The black shed was impossible to find at night unless you were looking for it, mostly because in addition to having a fresh coat of matte black paint on it, the damn thing was surrounded by dense trees and shrubs. It looked like a shitty little shed where cowboys could seek shelter from the rain. Inside, though, we had running water and a working drain. And a fresh coat of industrial paint. Extra glossy. "Stay close to the door."

Cruz nodded and followed a few feet behind me, giving me the time I needed to focus. "Call out if anyone approaches," he said to Romeo who nodded silently.

I stepped inside the shed, but couldn't see shit. It was pitch black. I groped on the wall until I flipped the switch to the only light inside the structure. A plain white bulb swinging from a chain. It was cliché as fuck, but it worked, startling the two men tied to chairs in the middle of the room, eyes covered with a blindfold.

The young one, Beto, wore a baseball jersey and the matching bandana tied around his head was stained with blood. The short, chubby dude in the other chair wore black slacks and dress shoes. What. The. Fuck?

I walked around them both, making sure my boots sounded heavy on the slick floor, stopping behind them. "Which one of you wants to talk first?"

"Fuck you," the chubby little one spat out, just like I knew he would.

"I guess that means you're the boss, right? The one with all the answers?"

Because he couldn't resist, Juno smiled. "Damn right I am, fucker."

LOADED

"Good." I walked around them and snatched the blindfold off Beto, meeting his gaze with my own. To his credit, the kid barely flinched. "When you get sick and tired of watching me beat the fuck outta your boss, you can tell me what I want to know. All right?"

He nodded because his boss couldn't see him.

"Beto, don't you say one fucking word."

I stood and cracked my neck, then my knuckles, because sometimes it was fun to terrorize an asshole. "Want to tell me why the fuck you shot up my club?"

Juno laughed and said, "Eat shit and die, motherfucker." Then my fist landed in the middle of his gut. "That's all you got?" he said, sputtering through blood coming out of his mouth.

I smiled, appreciating the ego of the classic tough guy even if it flew in the face of common sense, which he learned when I punched him twice, an uppercut and then a jab.

"Shit!" he finally whined.

"Is that jogging your memory at all?" I knew he wouldn't answer, would rather die than survive and have his men see him as weak. But I went through the motions because like my CO used to love saying, I had a hopeful heart. Always giving the subject too many chances to make a better decision. I didn't see it quite so charitably, but I couldn't deny that I got some pleasure from the violence of the process.

For thirty long, exhausting minutes, Juno refused to answer one fucking question, Worse than that, he was like a child, tossing out ridiculous insults. "Why don't you untie me, fucker? Or are all you white boys into this kinky shit?"

Another jab to the nose sent his head flying back as blood rushed down his face and throat, soaking his white shirt. A straight punch to his right jaw. His left. Another hit in the liver. "Why the fuck did you come back?"

The pain was getting to him because he was used to the way shit was done on the streets, a pure ass whooping until you either passed out or died. But this way, hitting multiple body parts over time, exhausted the subject everywhere, fatiguing the muscles and organs all at once. "Fuck. You."

I looked to Beto who seemed to be in shock, which meant he was new to the game. "No answer? Too bad." I unleashed another combination of punches and kicks until Juno could barely breathe.

"Maybe," he wheezed and then laughed, spitting out blood and taking a few deep breaths before trying to speak again. "Maybe we just wanted some kinky white boy sex. Since you sick fucks like to watch other dudes fuck your women, we figured we'd come get a taste of that willing pussy."

A punch to his side shut him up, and he passed out, not for long, but just enough to scare the fuck out of the kid. Juno's blindfold had come off and the kid couldn't miss the eye swollen shut or the giant split in his lip. He snapped his eyes shut and turned his head away.

"That crazy fucker who Ken was working for, Farnsworth is his name. But I don't know if it's his first or last name."

"Shut the fuck up!" Juno was back with us.

"Cruz, hand me that cattle prod, would ya?"

Juno froze, but Beto's eyes were still closed.

"He took Juno's kid sister, and he's holding her until this job is done."

There we go. Progress. "What job?"

"This shit, tonight. He said meet him in the parking lot of The Barn Door and gave us directions. Said to go inside and shoot the place up. Since he wasn't paying us and didn't give us a target, we just shot the place up."

Cruz slapped the ridged handle of the prod into my hand, and I took it instinctively, still processing what Beto had just said. "You weren't ordered to kill or capture anyone?"

"Nope."

LOADED

I thought about everything Peaches had said about Farnsworth. These guys were the best of the best, probably had no official identity and had been operating in the dark so long, they didn't know how to act any other way. Everything was an op and everyone a chess piece. And that's how it all came together. My feet were moving toward the door.

"Motherfucker!"

"Wait, where you going?" Juno's voice sounded behind me, and I stopped just outside the door, turning to the man with the eerie gray eyes and the neck tattoo.

"Romeo, right?"

"Unofficially, yeah. Just helpin' out."

"Bags on their heads and lights out. Keep an eye on them and someone will come check on you soon."

"Got it," he said, shoving his hands in his pockets and turning to do what I asked. He might make a decent prospect after all.

When Cruz caught up with me, I was already in the driver's seat on my phone.

"Gunnar, Farnsworth didn't just send them. He met them in the parking lot."

"It was just two gunmen, Wheeler." His voice was angry and annoyed.

"Wrong. Ford said three gunmen, and Beto said Farnsworth instructed them to meet him in the parking lot of the club. He was here on the property and they, fuck they were a distraction. Get to the house, Gunnar. Now!"

We were already on the move, heading towards the main house with our guns ready.

Chapter Fourteen

Annabelle

"Dr. Annabelle, wake up please." The soft distress in Maisie's voice pulled me abruptly from sleep, which I didn't mind because for some reason my mind was full of a certain blue-eyed vet and the wicked ways he lit up my body. "Please, Dr. Annabelle."

Maisie? Right. I opened my eyes; grateful the little girl hadn't flipped on the light because her sweet face in the moonlight was far more soothing.

"What's up, Maisie?" I sat up and swung my legs over the edge of the bed, taking in her little body in her princess nightgown and cowboy boot slippers.

"I'm thirsty, and I can't find Peaches." Her words were more whiny than worried, but I heard the worry and it instantly transferred to me. "Can you help me?"

"Of course, I can," I told her and scooped her up, enjoying the brief moment of having a kid in my arms before I set her on the bed. "Stay here." I grabbed a cup from the bathroom sink and filled it with the bottle of water on the nightstand, which was my attempt to keep out of everyone's way during my stay here. "Drink up."

"Thanks." She drank the water quickly and held it up for more. "Where is Peaches?"

I shrugged. "Probably somewhere kissing Gunnar." It was the safest answer and the most likely to be true, though the unease that settled in my gut wouldn't let me believe it. But it had the desired effect.

"Gross. They're always kissing."

"It's what grownups do when they love each other." I hoped I wasn't overstepping by saying that, but I knew Peaches would tell me if she had a problem with it.

"I know, but it's still gross."

"You won't always think so, kiddo." I ran a hand down her soft dark hair, for once missing her trademark pigtails. "Ready to get back to bed?"

She looked up at me and nodded. "Tell Peaches I couldn't find her, and I was afraid."

"I will," I promised and hugged her close for just a second, ignoring the unease that grew in my gut. After all the information that had been dumped on me in the past few days, it was hard *not* to think about the bad stuff, but Maisie didn't need to hear any of it. She didn't need to feel it coming from me or pick up any worry. "And I won't tell her about this late night party if you get to bed right now."

She smiled and scrambled off my lap and the bed, turning to give me her trusting little hand. "I'm ready now."

We walked hand in hand to the other side of the house where Maisie's bedroom sat just fifteen feet from the master suite. I tucked her in along with her favorite stuffed animal. "Anything else?"

"Just a hug and a kiss goodnight." She held her arms wide and expectant, so trusting it squeezed at my heart. I sent a wish up to the Gods or the universe or whoever was listening, that this feeling in my stomach was nothing more than my city nerves and neuroses.

"I can do that," I told her and dove in for a big hug and a smacking kiss on both of her cheeks. "How'd I do?"

"Perfect, Dr. Annabelle. Goodnight."

"Goodnight, sweetheart. Save me some coffee in the morning." She giggled and settled in, closing her eyes just as I pulled the door closed behind me, pressing my back against the door to settle my nerves.

The hall light flipped on and startled a gasp out of me. It was Gunnar, not the mysterious Farnsworth, but my heart still tried to beat its way out of my chest.

"Where's Peaches?" His frown was intimidating, but not more so than the way his wide shoulders seemed to expand with his anger.

"Good question," I said. I told him about Maisie's visit to my room. "I figured Peaches was downstairs working or worrying. I was headed down once I got Maisie back to bed." I stepped aside just in case he wanted to check on his baby sister. "I told Maisie you two were probably somewhere kissing."

A small grin twitched the corners of his mouth. "No. She's not downstairs either," he growled, and I could feel the worry emanating from his big body.

The door downstairs opened and closed loudly, a second before heavy, booted footsteps sounded on the wood entry, on a mission.

"Peaches?" Wheeler's voice was firm and strong and worried. "Fuck. All clear!"

It took my mind a few minutes to catch up since it was the middle of the night, but it was all starting to come together. Peaches wasn't home. No one knew where she was, and a crazy spy was after her. It didn't take a genius to figure out that this Farnsworth person had gotten to her.

"I didn't hear anything." It was a stupid thing to say, asinine really, but it was all I could manage as a sense of guilt overcame me. "I didn't hear a damn thing."

"My guess is that was his goal," Gunnar barked just as Wheeler stopped at the top of the landing. "Anything?"

"Her phone is on the counter." Their gazes connected, an unspoken communication that spoke of their bond, which I now understood, thanks to Peaches. These guys had gone through war together, and now they were living the after effects together. Rebuilding together. They were brothers in every way, and it was a bond I envied.

"Fucking Farnsworth. Has to be," Gunnar growled, practically pulling out his hair as he thought of the woman he loved in the hands of someone who meant to do her harm.

I didn't know much about any of this, but now that I knew more about Peaches, I understood better. Or at least I thought I did. "Check her phone."

Gunnar sighed and pushed off the wall. "Can't. She's got the fingerprint scan to get inside."

I laughed. "She made me do that for my phone, too. But I think Peaches was expecting something like this." I couldn't say why I thought it, just that I did.

"Are you saying she knew this was coming?"

"Of course not," I rushed to answer, ignoring the feel of Wheeler's glare on my back as we made our way downstairs to the kitchen. "But she got me to stay here by asking to help look after Maisie. She said having two sets of eyes at all times would be best. How could I say no to that?"

"What's that got to do with her phone?" Wheeler again, clearly that peaceful sleep hadn't done anything to cool his asshole tendencies, a fact I tucked away to examine later. Along with my disappointment at that fact.

"If she anticipated that Farnsworth would find a way to get to her, she would make it easy to get any helpful information we need." At their confused looks, I asked, "Haven't you ever played chess with Peaches? She's scary good." I'd love to watch her take down my father in a game, that's how good she was.

"No," Gunnar said angrily.

"Nope." Wheeler was unapologetic.

"Well fuck you both!" I didn't need them to validate my theory. I had working hands and legs, and I used them to get her phone and swipe my index finger across the lock screen. "It opened."

Gunnar grinned and took the phone offered. "Thanks, Doc."

"Annabelle," I said quietly, grateful I could offer anything that might help save my friend. "I'll keep an eye on Maisie. You guys find Peaches." My words were for both of them, but I refused to look at Wheeler even if my body leaned towards him, like a moth to a flame.

It was an unwanted attraction, and I was thankful there was something else to focus on right now.

Chapter Fifteen

Wheeler

Goddamn Farnsworth. Fuckin' MC. I swear there hadn't been one fucking moment of peace since either of those things entered my life. I wouldn't give up the MC for shit, the guys were my guys. My family, with the added bonus that my actual family was around, too, not that I ever paid attention to all the help my brother tried to give me. But this shit, the kidnapping of the Prez's girl, that shit was too fucking far.

And that's exactly why I'd dipped off into the kitchen inside the big house and grabbed a bottle of water to help me swallow down two of those Oxy's. It pissed me off, the way Annabelle had tossed them on the seat, so smug and sure that I wanted them. So confident that's why I'd come to her. But right now, even still pissed off at the presumption, I was grateful as fuck to her because I needed them. My leg was already throbbing like a motherfucker, probably because I slept in it after fucking Annabelle which I shouldn't have, and it would probably be another ten hours before I was in a position to remove it. So the pills would fill the gap, that was all.

Then I'd go back to being in pain and unable to sleep. But right now I needed to dull the pain so I could focus on what we needed to do to find Peaches and get her back.

"Toss me one too." Gunnar's deep voice pulled me from my thoughts and I grabbed another water bottle, tossing it to him.

"You should stay here." I knew saying that was asking for a fight, and I was grateful the rest of the MC was finishing up at The Barn Door and hadn't made it here yet.

"Fuck that. I'll be right by your side, leading these men when we go get my woman." He was anxious and angry and that's exactly what we didn't need going into a hot situation with a killer trained better than any of us. Probably even me.

LOADED

I sighed. It was exactly the answer I expected him to give, hell it was the answer I would've given if I gave a fuck about a woman enough to want to rescue her.

"Listen, Gunnar, we don't know shit about where he lives or where he would have taken her. To find those answers, we need you. Here."

He wasn't trying to hear me, but I needed him to, dammit. "You know Peaches in a way none of us do, which means you're the best person to go through that phone and surveillance equipment and tell us what will help."

"I don't know shit about how to do what she does, Wheeler. What the fuck good is that gonna do?"

"You know how to pull the surveillance footage up on her phone, and you probably know any passwords or codes to bypass any of her little boobytraps."

With reluctant agreement, he reached for Peaches' gold and pink sparkly phone case, which hid a high tech phone that was unlike any I ever saw at the mall cell phone store. He pulled up the surveillance footage, and I watched, over his shoulder, as a dark figure crept up to the side of the big house.

"That's about fifteen minutes into the shit show at The Barn Door."

"He planned well," I said, keeping my eyes on the intruder's movements. He favored his right side and couldn't be taller than six-foot-two, wearing all black. "He's coming from the west side of the property. Has to be Farnsworth." Even though his head was covered by a hoodie and all we could see were hands that belonged to a white male, I knew it was him.

"It could be any fuckin' body," Gunnar grumbled, too emotional to be useful right now.

"That's exactly how we know it's him, the fact that he could be anyone." I watched the video closely, clicking through each angle and playing the beginning again. The figure slipped around to the side of the house and, we assume, shimmied up to the side somehow.

LOADED

"That's where Maisie's room is!" Gunnar was on his feet right away, sending the bench flying backwards before it tipped over with a loud clatter. I stood and picked it up when his feet hit the stairs. He stomped to Maisie's room and then to the other end of the house to the guest suite where Annabelle was staying. Didn't take a genius to figure out what was going on. Still Gunnar came down, breathing a little easier. "She's cuddled up in Annabelle's room." He dropped back down with a sigh.

"Look at this. The light goes on in your room for a few seconds and then it goes out right away. About twenty seconds later the kitchen light comes on, you can see it from this angle," I switched to the back camera. "There!"

Another minute passed and then the door opened and Peaches emerged first, wearing an off-the-shoulder t-shirt and ratty old sweatpants, proof that asshole didn't even let her get dressed. Farnsworth is less than a foot behind her, the gun aimed at her back clearly visible on camera, as was the way Peaches kept a protective hand to her belly.

"She's pregnant."

It wasn't a question, I'd seen plenty of women in the desert who did the same thing when a bomb went off in the distance, or a car backfired. That protective mother's instinct kicked in like a motherfucker.

"Yeah, she is. You haven't noticed?" Gunnar arched a brow, his eyes lit with amusement for some reason.

I shook my head. "Can't say I pay a lot of attention to your woman's body, which I'm sure is banging. But no, I haven't noticed." I didn't bother to tell him that with the pills I wouldn't remember if I did notice.

"We haven't told anyone. We were gonna share it with you all, but then with all the Farnsworth shit, she was too freaked to even *think* about talking about it. She's been in big tops and loose pants for months." He shook his head as if just thinking about it stressed him out. "Imagine what that asshole would do if he knew?"

I nodded because I could imagine. There was a time I might have used that same info against an enemy. "Shit man, congratulations. You are happy right?"

"Happy as fuck. I didn't think I'd get this. I figured Maisie would be my only shot but now..." his big ass shit-eating grin said it all. "Now I'm gonna be a dad."

He smiled but it faded quickly. "Which is exactly why we have to my girl back and end this Farnsworth bullshit once and for all."

"We will, Gunnar, I promise. But we have to be smarter than Farnsworth, who's been trained by the best. Check her text messages," I said as soon as the thought came to me. "Peaches is the stubbornest damn woman I've ever come across, there's no way in hell she gave in to Farnsworth so easily, not when she knows better than any of us what he might have in store for her."

"You're right, dammit." His big fingers swiped through the thin phone furiously until he found what he was looking for. "Messages from an unknown number. Son of a bitch." He held up the phone, and I understood his frustration.

On the screen was a picture of Maisie, asleep in her bed, looking like an angel in her princess nightgown. The only thing that ruined the image was the gun aimed at her head. "Don't be stupid. Kitchen. 30 seconds."

"I'll kill him, Wheeler. I swear to fuck...I'm gonna kill that mother fucker!" There'd be no stopping him now that Farnsworth was dumb enough to threaten the little girl and take his pregnant lady.

"And I'll be right there, helping you reload. But until then, I need you to be cool. These guys love Peaches, and when we tell them, they're gonna lose their shit. All of 'em. Okay?"

He wanted to argue some more and I didn't blame him, but we didn't have time for that shit. "All right."

"Cool. Later you can fall apart and get shitfaced."

LOADED

The front door smacked open and the sound of different footsteps thunked against the hard wood floor. "Hey, yo, where is everybody?"

"Back here, Cruz!" He entered first, followed by Saint, Slayer, Holden and... "Mitch? What are you doing here?"

He shrugged. "I was unwinding at the club when everything happened. Figured I might be able to help, even if it's just keeping an eye on Maisie."

Gunnar nodded his appreciation. "Thanks man, have a seat."

Mitch gave me an odd look but kept his thoughts to himself while Gunnar and I caught the guys up on Peaches' kidnapping. "Any way to get this footage on the big screen?"

Gunnar shrugged, and Cruz groaned. "You bunch of fuckin' animals," he growled and took the phone from Gunnar's hand. A minute of messing with cords and shit, and the footage appeared on the fifty-inch TV, all four screens at once. "There."

"Is Doc around?" Saint held up his bandaged arm. "Figured she could take a look at it if she's around."

Gunnar nodded and sent Holden up, because Maisie knew him best.

Everyone watched in silence for the next fifteen minutes while my mind wandered all over the fucking place. Wondering how in the hell we would find Peaches and wondering how far we'd have to go to get her back. Not getting her back wasn't a fucking option. It would destroy Gunnar and probably send most of us on a suicide mission, which meant I couldn't let it happen.

We all had to be smart. Especially me, which was getting harder because maybe that second pill wasn't such a good idea. I hadn't eaten since earlier in the day, and I've been off the pills for the past week. But now I felt good, and there was a light haze around my vision.

"What do you think, Wheeler?"

Shit, I wasn't paying attention. "Come again?"

LOADED

"What the fuck?" Slayer scowled at me. "We boring you, man?"

"Just repeat what the fuck you said, Slayer. Save the bullshit for later."

Cruz, the natural born peacekeeper, stepped in. "Farnsworth would go somewhere nearby because Peaches won't be a quiet hostage. Or an easy one."

"Definitely." Shit, the pills were slowing me down.

"You all right, Wheeler?" That voice, so filled with concern and disappointment could only belong to my brother. "You don't look so hot."

"I look better than you," I told him with a smile.

"You're high." That prissy, accusing voice could only be one person.

"AB, nothing gets by you." My gaze slid to her, and I held in a groan at the way she looked, all sexy and sleep rumpled in her flannel shorts and long sleeve t-shirt.

"How many of those pills did you take, Wheeler?"

"What pills?" Mitch's concern was thick enough that I felt it hovering over me like a mother hen.

"Painkillers. The pain's been so bad he hasn't been able to sleep," Annabelle told him, breaking my confidence.

"*He's* right here," I slurred, at least I think it was me.

"He told you?" Mitch said.

She snorted. "I have eyes, Dr. Haynes." I imagined they were having one of those silent conversations, trying to figure out how to talk about my leg without being the one to break my confidence. "How many pills, Wheeler?"

I opened my eyes this time and scanned the room until I locked on those big brown eyes looking all concerned, like she had any right to be concerned about me. "Don't know what you're talking about, Doc."

She stiffened and then straightened her back. "Right, my mistake." Then she turned towards Saint. "You have a wound for me?"

"It's not a gift, Doc." Saint's disgruntled tone made her laugh, a pretty feminine sound I didn't get to hear nearly often enough.

"Says you. Let's go into the kitchen, and I'll get you fixed right up." She slid a glance at Mitch and then Gunnar before disappearing into the kitchen with Saint.

When they were gone, I felt Gunnar's stare on me. "What the fuck is going on, Wheeler?"

Uh oh, the Prez was pissed. "Nothin', just some pain. You know how it is." I didn't want to have this fucking conversation *ever* and damn sure not right now.

"No, Wheeler, I don't know how the fuck it is, so why don't you tell me?" Gunnar scraped both hands down his face as if doing so might erase some of the shit storm brewing around us. "Well?"

"The goddamn pain in my leg gets too bad if I've been on it all day," I told him and let out a long, exhausted breath. "And it's already been a long fucking day." With no ending in sight now that Peaches was gone. Missing. Kidnapped. That's when my words penetrated the fog of too many painkillers, and I realized I said too much.

Gunnar's glare never wavered. His nostrils flared in anger but it was the alarming shade of red on his face that spoke volumes about his current mental state. "Explain. Now."

Gunnar was pissed, but the rest of the guys were all looking at me with accusation burning in their eyes. Wondering if I was the man worthy of being Gunnar's second in command, if I could be trusted to have their backs when the shit hit the fan, which it had been doing a lot of lately. This was it, the moment to belong or keep myself apart from the group. Permanently.

There was no fucking decision in that, I realized. Hardtail Ranch was my home and these assholes, the Reckless Bastards, they were my brothers.

"Wheeler," Holden snapped, his patience thin.

LOADED

"Right." There was no easy way to reveal a secret I'd been hiding for so long. I scanned the living room and took a seat in the brown and gold chair beside the window and kicked out my left leg so when I leaned forward I could just tug up the leg of my pants.

"An IED went off on my last tour, killed my whole fucking team, and took my goddamn leg. The pain was getting so bad, so the Doc prescribed me some painkillers. I think I'm getting immune to them. She hasn't given me any in a while. So, I took some leftover pills to help make it through tonight because I knew you and Peaches needed me."

It didn't feel good, unloading all of my bullshit on these men who were already as scared as fuck about Peaches. Hell, for each other. On top of all that, they now had to worry about whether or not I was fit to do my fucking job. "You happy now? I don't know what the fuck else to say."

"Dude, how in the fuck do you keep a leg like that a secret for so long?" Slayer's question was equal parts disbelief and disgust. Before I could answer, he kept going. "We're your brothers, you dumb motherfucker."

The other Reckless Bastards nodded their agreement that I was less of an asshole and more of a jackass, a difference without distinction as far as I was concerned.

"It's not something I enjoy talking about. Most of the time I forget about it, because I want to forget about it. I'd love to forget that whole fucking day, but I can't. As the only survivor, it's my punishment to never, ever fucking forget."

"And if you need help while we're out at the club or taking care of business, how the fuck are we supposed to help?" Holden was more pissed than the rest of them, and I understood completely. He and I had grown close, talked about a lot of our baggage. A lot, but not all.

"Then I would have been shit outta luck, and I know it. I'm fucked up Holden, what the fuck do you want me to say?" Several tours and half a dozen off the books ops, a man was entitled to a little bit of fucked up and a whole lotta baggage. Right?

"Don't say shit, ever. As long as you don't give a fuck that we're going into battle with men you obviously don't trust."

That stung, and it wasn't fucking true. "That's bullshit and you know it." A quick glance around the room said that my so-called brothers agreed with Holden. Fuckers.

"Oh, so now we're going to act like I'm the only man in the club with problems? Big fucking problems," I said, my glance landing on Saint the moment he and Annabelle returned from the kitchen.

"Fine, I'm fucked up. I'm a liar." There was no point trying to argue with people who'd already made up their minds so I pulled my pant leg down, crossed my legs and looked out the window beside me, where the night had grown black except for the diamonds twinkling high and bright in the Texas sky.

"Thanks for sharing your secret with us," Gunnar said, his voice sincere.

"When you didn't have a fucking choice in the matter," Cruz added, doing a piss poor job of whispering.

Gunnar glared at him but said nothing. "Tonight, you stay here."

I wasn't surprised, but somehow, I was. "Why? Because you don't trust me?"

"Because I can't trust your reaction time when you're high on pain pills, and we need every man focused tonight." His expression was fierce as he readied himself to do battle, to go out and burn the world down, all to find his woman. "Besides, Maisie and the Doc will need some protection. Think you and Mitch can handle that?"

I gave a short nod, grateful the night and the revelation had gone much better than I could have ever imagined. I knew I had a lot to make up for, and I would start by keeping Maisie safe. Annabelle too.

Chapter Sixteen

Annabelle

Maisie had fallen asleep three hours ago, and I hadn't slept at all in that time. I couldn't. My mind wouldn't let me. It was too full of everything that had taken place earlier. I'd learned so much about Peaches, about the men now tasked with keeping me and the little girl pressed up against me, safe. The only thing I could focus on was just how little I knew about the people around me.

Peaches was some kind of government hacker or spy or something along those lines. The man I'd been sharing my body and my bed with was a biker and some kind of black ops specialist. I still didn't have all the details, which told me one thing: this wasn't where I belonged. If it was, I'd know a lot more about these people. I realized that even though I considered Peaches my best friend, it was clear that sentiment was not returned. We didn't have that kind of friendship, apparently. But those thoughts weren't helpful right now so I shoved them deep down and turned back to the present.

Peaches was kidnapped, very likely by some type of government g-man with no real name or birth certificate. Probably didn't even have any fingerprints. But she wasn't just kidnapped. I saw how she grabbed her stomach on the big screen TV when that man walked her out. She was pregnant. And considering my friend's sassy mouth, there was a good chance she'd get hurt—or killed. I couldn't think about that right now because the only thing I could do to help was keep this little girl safe.

Maisie slept peacefully, her body snuggled up to mine with such confidence. Such trust. Her right arm and right leg were flung across my midsection, her head resting on my shoulder while her long hair hung across my neck. She was such a sweet little kid, so trusting and precocious and certain in the love of every adult in her orbit.

LOADED

I would do everything I could to make sure she remained in that sweet, happy bubble. But sleep wouldn't come, and if I lie here awake any longer, all the moving around would wake her. Since I hadn't heard a bunch of bikes descend on the ranch yet, I figured we were still alone. I slid my feet into slippers and checked the window before creeping, quietly, downstairs. The small creaks and squeaks kept my nerves on edge.

Tea. Definitely tea and maybe some of Martha's cookies would relax my mind enough that I could get a few hours of sleep in before Maisie woke up. Without sleep I wouldn't be focused and without that focus I couldn't keep my word to Peaches. I couldn't keep Maisie safe. So...cookies and tea.

The kitchen was dark aside from the light above the stove. It shed just the perfect amount of light on a night like this where the stars and the moon were shining bright. That and too much light would make it easy to see right inside the windows. A big figure with wide shoulders sat shrouded in black, hunched over the kitchen table, startling the crap out of me.

"Oh, shit! Wheeler? Are you okay?"

Obviously not, since he was sitting in the dark. Completely quiet. But I knew, even before I asked the questions, he wouldn't share a damn thing with me.

"You know I'm not," he said without even turning to look at me. "You made damn sure of that, didn't you?"

"Right," I snorted. "It's all *my* fault you've got problems you refuse to share with anyone, even your own damn brother. You have pain that you refuse to address unless or until it's convenient for you. But sure Wheeler, blame it all on me."

What difference did it make? Wheeler would believe what he wanted no matter what I said or did. So I busied myself making a cup of basil and lemon tea to go with the pineapple upside down cake I found in the oven, slapping a slice of cheddar on top before popping it into the microwave. It was a treat I hadn't let myself enjoy since medical school.

"Gross," Wheeler snorted when I set the plate and saucer on the table across from him.

"It's a good thing I didn't offer you any, then." He was looking for a fight and I wasn't in the mood, not with some psycho out there doing who knew what to Peaches.

"Maybe, but now my curiosity is piqued, and I want a bite." He leaned forward, revealing that too handsome face with sparkling blue eyes as a slow smile spread across his mouth.

"Maybe I'll save you a bite," I told him disingenuously. There was no way that anyone was getting even one little sliver of this amazing treat. My mouth watered even thinking about taking a bite. I looked at him closely, noticing the tension around his eyes and mouth. "Seriously Wheeler, how are you feeling?"

He shrugged, thinking about bullshitting me I was sure, but I was happy in the end he didn't. "The pills wore off hours ago, but the pain has been hovering somewhere around a six."

I nodded, biting back at least ten different responses before I settled on one. "For the love of God, Wheeler, take off the damn prosthetic. You've told everyone the truth so stop being a baby." As a physician, it went against everything I believed in to be so callous to someone so clearly in pain, but the man was damn infuriating. He would rather let the pain kill him than admit to having a weakness.

"Easy for you to say," he grunted in his usual disgruntled tone.

"Actually it's not. You think it's easy for me to sit here and watch you in pain when I know how much you're suffering? Well, it's not, dammit."

I sipped on my tea and turned my gaze to the cake. "Do what you want, you will anyway." One thing I'd learned in dealing with my father, other physicians, and patients in the medial field, was that people did what they wanted, regardless of professional advice, past history, or common sense. In that aspect, Wheeler wasn't so different than the average man.

We sat in silence for so long that it almost became comfortable. Almost, but nothing could ever be classified as comfortable, not with the underlying current of dark desire that arced between us whenever we were together. "It was my fault. I didn't see the IED."

I had to search my memory bank for what the acronym stood for and I nodded when I remembered, saying nothing. But I remembered seeing photos of bodies mangled and injured by those explosive devices. It wasn't pretty, but it gave me some clue about what Wheeler had gone through.

"I was too distracted by my own goddamn biases to realize that the pregnant teen and her brother served as the perfect distraction. My mind was on her, wondering if she was the woman we were looking for, or just another teenager gobbled up into an ancient system that didn't fucking respect women. All of that. I was fucking thinking all of that, while they were setting us up." He looked so damn despondent, so helpless and equally hopeless. His blue eyes had paled as he spoke and taken on a faraway look that broke my heart. "By the time I focused back on the present, chaos had taken over."

I listened to his story and his words stuck with me, they hit me, each and every one of them like a bunch of tiny little knives. The words that hurt the most were the ones that stuck with Wheeler, the way he thought about that day. "It must have been horrific for you, Wheeler. I'm sorry."

"Yeah, me too," he grumbled, and I slid my mug of tea over to him. "Fat lot of fucking good it does me now though, with my whole crew dead and buried. Me here, barely alive and not even a whole man."

"That wasn't your fault, Wheeler." If he believed nothing else, I hoped he believed that. "Once you saw those kids on the side of the road, things could only play out the way they did."

"You can't know that. You can't fucking know that, AB." His large hand smacked against the table, making me gasp in surprise. "You can't know that," he said, this time softer. Quieter. More resigned.

"Not for sure, no. There's no way to know things like this for certain, but I know those people had a plan and it was to distract you. Where you see it as a weakness, I see a strength. They used the one thing that we all know and admire about men like you."

"What's that," he asked, cynicism dripping from both sharp syllables.

"That you're a good man with a kind heart. That you wouldn't hesitate to turn your attention to a teen mom and a little boy, to make sure they were all right, stranded in the middle of a war zone. They used that against you, Wheeler, and you couldn't change that any more than you can choose your eye color."

His gaze said he was unconvinced. "Nice interpretation, Doc."

It was no use. Nothing I said would penetrate his thick skull and definitely not when his mind and heart were full of guilt, anger, and fear. I knew when to give up and go regroup, so I stood and rinsed my plate before setting it in the sink the way Martha preferred. I gave it once last shot before turning in.

"It's always how you interpret things, Wheeler. For example I could choose to see you as an asshole who used me to get pills. Instead, I choose to see you as a man in such tremendous pain that he didn't care who he hurt to get what he needed. Because of those incredible orgasms, I'm not holding it against you." I patted his shoulder, appreciating his dumbfounded look. "Get some sleep, pretty boy. You look terrible."

He let out a shocked grunt, but for once, Wheeler said nothing. I made my way back upstairs where I checked the window again and slid under the blankets and enjoyed a few more full hours of sleep before the thundering sound of motorcycle engines tore through the night air.

Chapter Seventeen

Wheeler

"Well?" It was a loaded question, but with everyone gone all damn night, I was a nervous wreck. I had to know what they found out. Instead of answering my question, Slayer and Saint grabbed food from plates and platters the moment Martha set them on the table. For her part, the housekeeper was fluttering around like the kitchen was on fire, whipping up food as fast as we could inhale it. The kitchen looked like a holiday with the table piled high with scrambled eggs, pancakes, sausage, bacon, fruit and for some strange reason, mac & cheese.

"Well, goddammit?"

Slayer stopped shoveling in his toast-bacon-scrambled eggs sandwich into his mouth and stared at me.

"Well, what, Wheeler? If that's even your real name," he mumbled and went back to his fucking sandwich.

"Asshole." So he was still mad. *They* were all still mad about the secret I'd kept from them, and I understood that, even if I thought it was a secret I had every fucking right to keep. "Whatever." If this was how it was gonna be from here on out, it was just fine with me. Just fucking fine.

Cruz chose that moment to stroll into the kitchen with sleepy blue eyes and a wide smile on his face. He wrapped both arms around Martha's plump form and smacked a kiss against her cheek.

"Miss Martha, mac & cheese for breakfast? You beautiful woman, are you trying to get me to propose to you? Because I will." Martha tittered like a woman half her age while her daughter, Evelyn, who'd been subdued since the death of her twin sister, merely snorted her disgust.

"Get outta here, Cruz. I'm old enough to be your grandmother." She swatted his arm and then his behind when he moved too quickly for her.

"Maybe," he told her laughing and wiggling his eyebrows suggestively. "Or maybe I like my women aged, just like a fine wine." Martha laughed again and dumped more eggs from an oversized skillet onto another big plate and took it to the table.

"Martha's too smart to fall for your lies, brother." Saint's words came out quiet, damn near inaudible, but sometimes, he opened up and became less withdrawn.

Cruz sat down and piled a base layer of mac & cheese on his plate before adding the rest of the food Martha had laid out. "Martha is the only woman I'll never lie to. She knows that." He batted his eyelashes at her and again, the old woman blushed all the way down to her toes.

"What a lucky gal," Holden deadpanned from the far end of the table.

Gunnar's appearance sucked all the kidding and even some of the oxygen from the room. His boots smacked hard against the floor with every step, making it impossible to ignore him. "So what do we know?"

I held back a grunt at the fact that the same goddamn question had gone unanswered when I asked. I was just as pissed off as they were, apparently, so I kept my fucking trap shut and listened. I could help find Peaches, that much was certain. Anything after that, well I guess we'd all just have to wait and see.

"I talked to the old girls at the B&B over a plate of lemon and lavender cookies," Slayer said, patting his flat belly at the memory. "They recall a man, not from around here, asking questions. They pegged him for a cop or PI but he matches Farnsworth's description, which is to say fucking non-descript."

Saint nodded, talking around buttery toast. "Hazel said the same thing. A few of the guests last night mentioned that a PI had been asking questions."

Gunnar arched his brows, suspicion rolled off him. "The guests just happened to bring it up?"

Saint sighed and rolled his eyes. "Some lady was hitting on Haze, and she was *unaware*." He hesitated on that last word, and I wasn't the only one who noticed. Gunnar and Slayer both leaned in, and I was sure he could feel Holden's glare like a laser. "Anyway, she used the opportunity to her—to *our*—advantage and made up a story about how she thought some guy was hitting on her in town but it turns out he was a PI."

Slayer and Cruz both laughed. "Quick on her feet, that one," Cruz said, proudly.

"The women clocked his description, plain but good looking, and mentioned they'd all fallen for it too. That's it." Saint's voice was firm, telling even Gunnar that he wouldn't take any shit about Hazel getting the MC valuable intel. "Point is, he's definitely living in town and asking a lot of vague questions."

Cruz chugged back a full mug of coffee and slammed it down with a grin. "Big Mac said he thought maybe squatters had taken up residence over at Early Healey's place because Lorna the realtor hadn't gotten the commission on it, and she's the only realtor in town." He rolled his eyes and I could only imagine how much time it took to get that information from the chatty old man. "He would've gone to check it out himself but after all that shit that's been happening in Opey, he figured he'd just pass the info along."

"Mr. Non-descript didn't ask one question about Peaches?" That was the strangest fucking part of all. We all knew she was the target even before he'd brazenly come onto the ranch and took her, so why not get all the gossip from the people of Opey?

A chorus of "No" went around the room, increasing the frustration by a factor of ten.

"That is fucking weird," Slayer growled and bit into a biscuit like it was a piece of raw meat. "Are we just wasting our time, man? Is this some psyops type shit?" His question was aimed at me, I realized after a long moment.

"Could be, but I wouldn't draw that much attention to myself. You get people talking, especially a certain type of people and eventually they'll tell you what you want to hear."

LOADED

"So they all probably told him bits and pieces about all of us? The ranch? The club? The MC?"

I nodded at Gunnar's rapid fire questions rather than repeat myself. "Ask Cruz what else he learned from Big Mac."

Cruz groaned. "Please, don't. My brain is so full of who's sneaking off at lunchtime with his secretary and so much gossip that goes on in this town. I won't fucking do it." He reached out and shoved a biscuit, sandwiching bacon and sausage into his mouth for good measure.

"Point taken," Gunnar grunted, still barely looking at me. "Slayer and Cruz, I want you to go check out Healey's place just before sunset. Take a look around and leave your *kuttes* and bikes at home."

Both men nodded and I swear they barely resisted the urge to stand and salute, such was Gunnar's pull on men.

"Holden, you and Saint make sure the club is cleaned up and ready. You guys will work the club and keep an eye on things. Hazel too, since she's so good at it." His lips twitched which seemed to sooth Saint's instantly ruffled feathers.

Holden grunted at the idea of working the club again, but he knew it could be worse if he said anything. "I call bar," he said loudly, gaze directed at Saint.

"Fine by me." The gleam in Saint's eye said he was happy to roam the club and watch all the fucking and freakiness that went on inside those walls and dozens of rooms. "You can keep an eye and ear on Hazel."

"Lucky me," he grunted and that seemed to ease some of the tension in the kitchen. We'd all been on the receiving end of Hazel's harassment as I liked to call it. The woman had a knack for riling us up, for finding our buttons and pressing them until we cracked. Then she'd smile and laugh and say, *see that wasn't so bad was it?* And the worst of it was? She was usually right.

"See if Mitch is willing to pitch in too." I didn't know if that meant he trusted me to keep the girls safe on my own or if he planned to stick around to chaperone me.

LOADED

The back door smacked open and everyone drew their guns and aimed, instinctively. "Aspen," Holden growled. "What the fuck?"

"Sorry, babe" she heaved, out of breath with her hands in the air.

"Guns down!" Holden's growl was primal and we all holstered our pieces. "Babe, seriously?"

She shrugged. "I woke up to get some water and when I checked the time, I saw your message. I figured this was a *time is of the essence* type deal and came right over." Aspen strolled in, eyes on all the food at the table until she found an empty glass and a carafe of juice. She drank half a glass and leaned against the counter. "I found this last night when I was going through all the junk I cleaned from Ken's old condo," she said and held up a phone. "And this." A thick red envelope.

"What is it?" Gunnar's impatience was palpable.

Cruz snatched the phone from her hand and immediately began to mess around with it. "I'm not Peaches, but I'll see if there's anything I can find."

She handed the photos to Gunnar who looked at each one and passed it along. "Looks like Ken was doing some of his own recon."

When the photos made their way to me, I had to agree. "That's a different Farnsworth, right?"

"Holy shit," was Cruz's stunned reply. "How did I not see that shit?"

Aspen nodded. "It's like walking into a waiting room for an audition. Everyone looks exactly the same but *slightly* different."

"Yep. Most of the photos are of the current Farnsworth," I confirmed.

"And these here are of the asshole who came to the house when Maisie and I first got to the ranch." Gunner said.

I knew this wasn't the time to bring it up, but Gunnar and Peaches had been tightlipped about their trip. "This have anything to do with what you found or didn't find in New York?"

Gunnar glared, but I knew he wouldn't hold back. "We didn't find jack shit. The place had been scrubbed, like *ghost in the fucking night* kind of scrubbed. No fingerprints or any trace that anyone had been there and everything was pristine like a model home." He blew out a breath and took a big gulp of coffee. "Peaches did find something, but she refused to share it with me. Said it would put me in too much danger and maybe get her put in prison. Now I wished I'd fought her about it, dammit."

I had to snort at that. "We both know you could've fought until you were blue in the face, and she wouldn't give in if she thought it would hurt you. Or the MC. But she's not here, which means we need to go through her digital shit, all of it, to see if we can find anything that tells us any goddamn thing about why he took her and where."

Gunnar nodded. "Agreed, but not now. Later. Everyone get some goddamn rest and meet back here at six. I'm gonna sleep and spend some time with my little sister."

Everyone finished eating and dispersed to their separate homes, including me. I limped my way back to the bunkhouse to get this fucking leg off for a few hours.

Chapter Eighteen

Annabelle

I knew it was a bad idea. I knew it just as well as I knew how to stop a gunshot wound from bleeding, yet I stood there on the other side of Wheeler's door with my fist poised to knock. Only I didn't knock, not yet. I sucked in a deep breath and reminded myself that Wheeler was a man who was suffering. Experiencing a type of pain most of us could never imagine, both mental and physical. Finally, I knocked. And waited.

"Come in, Annabelle." His reply was quiet and anguished.

I opened the door and bit down on the inside of my jaw at the sight he made, lying on the bed shirtless with the sheet draped temptingly across his lower abdomen. "How did you know it was me?"

His blue-eyed glance cut over to me, but the rest of him was stock-still. "The guys don't knock, and

Maisie knocks as she's opening the door and letting herself in." He shrugged. "Who else could it be?"

So predictable. "Oh." There was nothing to be said when a man called you predictable. *Boring*.

"What's up?" His gaze raked over my body, as strong as any caress.

I had to suppress a shiver at the heat in his eyes. "How are you feeling?"

"Not great, Doc." He grunted, and his skin was pale, coated in a sheen of sweat upon closer inspection. "Wanna give me something?"

My shoulders sank at his words, even though they didn't surprise. Maybe a small part me of hoped he was done with them or at least done asking me for them. "Do you *need* something, Wheeler?" If he wanted them, he'd have to ask outright this time. No more hinting and beating around the bush so he could hit me with the old 'I never asked you for anything' when it suited him.

LOADED

The blue in his eyes seemed to darken with every passing second until I could feel his every dirty thought skitter across my skin. "I need a lot AB. A whole lot."

"Like?" I asked, my voice and my body both vibrating with need.

"For starters, you." He reached out and pulled me, until I was on top of him and our bodies were completely aligned. "Stay right here," he grunted. "I like the feel of you on me."

I snorted because we both knew that wasn't true. "You're in pain," I insisted.

He grinned and smacked my ass, gripping each cheek tight. "You're gonna be my pain reliever, Annabelle." Then his lips were on mine in slow, drugging kiss that had my toes curling in my slippers. His lips were firm, insistent that they lead the dance he took us on. It was slow and sensual, a give and take of his lips and his tongue, giving me immense pleasure and then taking it all back, before giving it back five-fold.

I tore my lips from his and sucked down a lot of air, chest heaving and my eyes wide because I could not believe that kiss had just happened. And because I wanted more of it. A whole lot more. "Dammit, Wheeler."

His deep chuckle vibrated my whole body until my toes curled once again, and I arched into him. "I know, AB. I find you irresistible too."

"You want me." It wasn't a question. I could feel just how much he wanted me pressing right up against the thin silk of my panties. I didn't need him to want more or to pretend there was a possibility for more, because I wanted him. *Badly.*

"I do, AB. So bad I want to taste it. All of it." He licked his lips as they curved into a satisfied smile, and his hips flexed against mine.

"Then I'm in charge," I told him. I wanted him, but I didn't want him to put that damn leg back on just so we both could get our freak on, so I stayed where I was and gazed down at him. "Don't argue with me."

LOADED

"It's a good thing I'm naked under this sheet, AB." His hands went to my hips and scraped up my waist to my breasts, squeezing and playing with my nipples until he tugged a cry from my lips. "That's the sound I want to hear." He squeezed again and this time I arched into his touch and moaned, again. "That sound hits me right in the cock."

His crude words brought a smile to my face. I continued to slid up and down the ridge of his cock, moaning as my panties grew wetter and wetter. "Wheeler."

"Fuck, Annabelle." He gripped my hips and thrust against me until I screamed out my pleasure.

I couldn't take it anymore, I pulled back in sharp jerky motions, yanked down the sheet and fisted his cock, pumping up and down, hard until his hips thrust up against me. "Your cock always gets so hard for me, Wheeler." His hips thrust again and I smiled, sliding my panties to the side and lowering myself on his impressive cock.

"Oh, fuck! Yes!" I rode his cock like I was headed towards the finish line, which in a way I guess I was. He was hard and thick inside of me, hips rising up to meet mine with every thrust. It was wicked and delicious, and I bit down on his shoulder to avoid waking up the rest of the house. "Wheeler."

"You ride so good." He held my hips with a firm grip and pounded into me like the answers to all of life's questions could be found in there. "Fuck!" His teeth clenched hard, but he couldn't get the leverage he needed so I took over.

"I'm in charge," I growled and put my hands to his chest, pressing him down into the plush mattress as I began to ride him, harder and faster, so hard that he sank as deep as he could get. Deep enough to make me tremble mid-stride. "Oh fuck yes!"

"AB," he growled again, hands snaking down to my ass in a firm grip, guiding our speed. "Fuck!"

I leaned forward and sank my teeth into the that little tendon between his shoulder and his neck, using his chest to take more of him, to change the angle at which we came together. It felt so good, so damn right that I couldn't stop the pleasure as it barreled down on me. On him. It shot out of every pore and I couldn't stop the long, tortured cry. "Oh my God!"

Wheeler grabbed my face, tight enough to sting, his grip firm. "Just me, Wheeler. Not God." He flashed a sultry smile and fused our lips together, kissing me deeply as he buried his cock deeper and deeper, around my orgasm.

"Fuck, you feel so goddamn good." He surged up and shuddered before flipping me onto my back.

"Feel better?"

He nodded. "A hell of a lot better. Thanks, Doc."

I froze at that casually tossed out 'Doc' because I knew what he was doing, and I knew why, but it still pissed me off. There was no point going over it all. Again. I got dressed and left without a word. We both got what we wanted and after a quick shower, I'd have a hot cup of coffee warming my bones from that instant chill.

The kitchen was thankfully empty since even Martha hadn't come back from the servant's quarters after breakfast. Even though I heard them all talking downstairs, I stayed up in my own room with my thoughts. They had a lot of MC business to discuss and it had nothing to do with me at all. I was here to look after Maisie, that was it.

Alone with my thoughts and a second mug of coffee, I sat at the table and sent a prayer to anyone who might be able to control any part of this life, to keep Peaches safe. Maisie needed her and that baby she carried, to give her a full and happy life after all the loss she'd already suffered. I would keep that suffering to a minimum as much as I could, while I was here.

A knock on the back door pulled me from my thoughts with the force of a hurricane. My heart thudded as my flight-or-fight instincts kicked in, I scanned the kitchen in search of a weapon. A proper weapon. My eyes landed on the knives first. They were practical but required close combat. Then my gaze landed on a shotgun leaning up against the wall behind the door. I wrapped my hand around the handle and tucked it under my arm, slowly pulling the door open with my free hand.

A woman stood on the porch with shoulder-length pink hair, a small baby bump and a smile on her face. "You must be Dr. Annabelle Keyes. I've heard a lot about you."

I blinked, wondering who in the hell this woman was and if I needed to shoot her or invite her in. "Uhm, do I know you?"

She laughed. "Sorry I'm Vivi." She held out a hand, which I accepted while her words sank in. Vivi. "Peaches has a way of painting a picture and you are every bit the pretty country doctor she described."

I wanted to spend some time on the whole 'country doctor' thing but we didn't have time. "Peaches isn't—"

"Here? I know. That's why I'm here. When she didn't check in I knew something was up, and I'm here to get my girl back."

Instantly I liked her. She seemed brash and outgoing, strong and capable. And Peaches had confirmed that she was a certified badass. "Come on in."

Chapter Nineteen

Wheeler

I woke up hours after Annabelle left my room feeling good. Hell, I felt better than good, well-rested, energized and ready to crack some skulls to get Peaches back if that was what it took. I didn't know what prompted Annabelle to say yes, but I was goddamn glad she had because being buried inside her was intoxicating. Watching her and gripping her hips while she rode my cock, back arched so her tits were just a tongue flick away, and the fucking sounds she made. I got hard just thinking about it again.

Fuck. It shouldn't feel so good to want the wrong woman as badly as I wanted Annabelle, but dammit I did. And I was unapologetic about it. She was prissy, but she was hot. And freaky. And the way she craved my cock made me feel ten feet tall.

But now wasn't the time to be thinking about my sexy little doctor. Now was the time to think about getting the Prez's girl back. I jumped into a hot shower and got dressed, making a beeline for the coffee I didn't really need but wanted. Desperately. That and I wanted something hot in my hands when I spoke to Gunnar. Part of the reason I'd gotten up early was to have a few words with him before the rest of the guys arrived.

"Good afternoon, ladies." Maisie sat at the table, munching on a sandwich and some of Martha's homemade potato chips. Her vegetables remained untouched and a small milk moustache covered her top lip.

"Wheeler, I got chips!" She held up one thin sliced potato and bit into it with the gusto only a little girl could manage in the middle of a crisis.

"Can I have some?"

"Miss Martha made plenty of them, didn't you?"

Martha stood at the stove pulling more chips from the hot oil with some wide wire thing. "Sure did. I'll get some on a plate for you, Wheeler."

LOADED

"Thanks." I grabbed one of the oversized mugs Martha kept around for the ranch hands and filled it with coffee before taking the seat across from Maisie. "How's it going kid?"

"All right." She sighed as if the weight of the world was on her shoulders. "I miss Peaches."

I didn't know what, if anything, Gunnar had told her about Peaches' absence. I didn't want to step on any landmines while I was already in the doghouse, so I said, "I do too, kid, even though she always gives me shi—a hard time. But don't tell her I said that." I pointed an accusing finger her way, and she erupted in a fit of giggles that made it impossible not to smile.

"I won't. I promise." She took a monster bite from her sandwich before asking her next question. "When is she coming back?"

"No clue," I told her honestly. "But I plan to find out, kid. Be good for Martha."

"I will! Dr. Annabelle says we're gonna have a tea party when she gets back from the hospital."

239

I froze in the doorway and turned, asking my next question as calmly as I could, even as my thoughts churned. "Why did she go to the hospital?" Gunnar had impressed upon her the need to stick close to Hardtail Ranch until Peaches came back safe, so why the hell was she ignoring that?

"There was an accident on the interstate," Martha explained. "Needed every available hand. Gunnar sent Saint with her," she added with a twinkle in her eye.

"Thanks." I grunted like it was Martha's fault that Gunnar had sent Saint and not me. Still, it was another kick to the nuts. Yet another kick landed on the family jewels when I stepped into Gunnar's office and found more than half the MC already there.

Cruz leaned against the bookshelf with his arms folded over his chest while Holden stood tall with his shoulders squared, expression deadly serious. Slayer perched on one edge of the desk; legs crossed at the ankle. "I'd ask if I missed anything but it seems like that's exactly the point."

LOADED

Gunnar stood and crossed his arms. "Figured you could use the rest."

Sleep it off was more like it, but no one bothered to say it, because it was all bullshit anyway. "Right. Anything I should know?"

Gunnar gave a sharp nod, and I didn't miss the look of relief when I changed the subject. "Managed to get some aerial eyes on Healey's property, thanks to Vivi, here."

He nodded to the pregnant woman with the pink hair curled up on the sofa behind the door.

"Looks like someone is in there but we don't know who or how many, so we'll wait for Slayer and Cruz to get eyes on the tenants."

I gave the woman a nod of greeting before getting back down to business. "Did you find anything Peaches might have kept hidden, thinking she was protecting Gunnar?"

I could have prettied up the words but there was no time for that shit and pink hair glared at me. "Not yet. What about you, Master Sargent Haynes? Don't you have some *connections* you can tap into to get info on Farnsworth?" Her smug, taunting gaze remained on me, unwavering in the certainty that she'd gotten me.

She had and that wasn't even the worst fucking part. No the worst fucking part was the fact that I hadn't thought of it myself. I was too busy feeling sorry for myself that I might've lost the trust of the MC to focus on what mattered and that was using every tool at our disposal to get Peaches back.

"I'll see what I can find, *Vivi*," was all I said, and I got the fuck away from everyone.

The calls I needed to make were private, and I needed some way to fortify my nerves before rising from the dead and reaching out to those still living. Still fighting.

Chapter Twenty

Annabelle

Motor vehicle accidents were the worst kind of emergencies, even worse than gunshots. Bullets tore through flesh and did unspeakable damage to human organs and bones, but the pain and torture an automobile could inflict was unimaginable. Not for me, of course, because I'd spent the past twelve hours inside one operating room or another, patching up a variety of body parts. All thanks to some truck driver who decided to skip his required resting time and fell asleep behind the wheel. That one decision, that one act had changed the lives and futures of more than two dozen people.

It was a life lesson we could all use, me in particular. It was time to stop doing things—and people—who made me feel like shit. Time to stop fooling myself about Wheeler and what I felt for him. Time to stop pretending I didn't know about all the illegal shit going on at Hardtail Ranch. Every decision I made, or willfully choose *not* to make had an impact on my life. Positive or negative, nobody knew, but making a choice had to better than letting the choice make itself. Right?

"You all right, Dr. Keyes?" Tish's voice was always full of maternal concern and today even her face was softened in sympathy.

"I'm good, Tish. Just a really long day. Really long." Four fatalities out of sixteen injured was too much, but those numbers said nothing of the three who had died *en* route to the hospital. "You holding up okay?"

"Yeah," Tish said. "Days like this are always hard, but I go home and hug my kids extra tight and kiss my husband like we're teenagers again, and it makes it all a little less terrible."

"Sounds nice," I told her absently, barely able to keep my eyes open as I sat behind my desk. "I just need to finish the report for that last lung puncture and then

LOADED

I'm headed home. Go get a jump on making out with your hubby."

She grinned and with a small finger wave, left me to my thoughts, which were, honestly, all over the place.

They swirled so much I dozed off for a few minutes, waking with a start at the slam of a locker down the hall in the employee locker room. It was time to get back to the ranch and hopefully get a few hours of sleep. If I had known what the day had in store for me, I would've used those early morning hours a bit more efficiently. But I wasn't thinking about Wheeler, not today. Not anymore.

Instead, I gathered my things, my jacket, and the bag that contained a change of clothes as well as emergency medical supplies.

The bag knocked over one of many boxes stacked around my office. Most days I would have just left it until my next shift since I didn't share the space with anyone, but a shiny object drew my attention. It was a tape recorder, which was odd, not just because it was about fifteen years out of date but because it didn't belong to me. I'd given up the old school recorder in med school, opting for the digital version instead because I could get notes done anywhere I wanted.

The cassette deck wouldn't open so I pressed each of the buttons, letting the nostalgia wash over me as each button clicked up when the previous was one depressed. On the record button, I hit pay dirt. A long red metal object jutted from the battery section of the recorder. I pulled it until I recognized the object.

A flash drive. "Holy shit a...*flash drive*," I whispered the last two words to myself, just in case someone was listening.

Then I remembered my shadow. Saint. I shoved the flash drive into the pocket of my scrubs. I had time to think about what to do first. Obviously, I would tell Gunnar and Vivi what I found, but the question was, should I take a peek before then?

Peaches' words came back to me, not to mention her current predicament. What if viewing whatever was on the drive was more dangerous than I realized?

LOADED

What if it put me in more danger? Or Peaches? Or Maisie? Suddenly even possessing the damn thing made me nervous. I wondered if I had it in me to put the flash drive back and pretend I'd never seen it.

I could do that, couldn't I? Maybe it wasn't from Peaches. Maybe some of my father's stuff had gotten mixed up with mine. That was plausible. Completely.

If I didn't examine it, or my own moral compass too closely.

"Dammit."

"Hey Doc, you all right?"

Saint's voice pulled me from my thoughts once again, and I flashed an overly bright smile that had his brown eyebrows raising in concern. "I'm fine, Saint, thanks for asking. Days like this take a lot out of me."

He nodded. "I know what you mean. Want to stop for a drink before heading back to the ranch? There won't be any peace there anytime soon."

That sounded wonderful, but everyone in town had heard about the pile up by now, and they would all want details, offer up sympathies or gossip about the trucker, none of which I was in the mood for at the moment.

"Thanks for the offer but curling up in bed sounds even better."

Saint nodded and fell into step beside me, offering up the kind of mindless small talk that didn't require too much brainpower until we reached his SUV.

I was grateful because it kept my mind off Wheeler and his constant efforts to keep his walls up around me. And it most certainly kept me from thinking about the tiny stick currently burning a hole in my pocket.

"That wasn't too painful, was it?" he said as we headed back to the ranch.

"It was a good attempt at blending in with the citizens of Opey," I told him on a laugh.

"Gee, thanks Doc."

"Anytime. How's the wound?"

LOADED

"Clean and starting to heal, I promise. Hazel loves playing nurse."

"Too much information," I told him, making the biker flush pink and stumble over his words.

"I did mean it like that, Dr.—"

"I know, Saint." I said as we pulled up to the ranch house. "It was my attempt at humor, a poor one it turns out." Add lacks a sense of humor to my list of attributes that have all the single men vying for my affection. "Thanks for being my bodyguard today."

"Anytime." He killed the engine, stepped out of the car and slammed the door behind him, leaving me alone once again with my thoughts. This time they had little to do with Wheeler and more to do with if I really wanted to know what was on that drive.

A knock on the window startled me, and I turned to see Vivi grinning, an amused expression on her face. "I hear if you stare at the house long enough, you'll be transported inside."

"I wish," I told her and stepped from the passenger seat, grabbing my bag as we both made our way up the steps. "Just trying to decompress after a long day. How are you?"

"Fine, fine. Tired and hungry and needing to pee a lot sooner than I did with my first kid. Wanna talk about it?"

I frowned. "About the baby pressing on your bladder?"

"No," she rolled her eyes. "Whatever put the shadow in your eyes?"

I appreciated the offer but I handled my work grief on my own, usually with a long hot bath and a bottle of wine. "No thanks. It's just a typical day at work, only with more customers."

"Bullshit, but the offer stands for as long as I'm in town." It was a nice gesture.

"I see why Peaches loves you so much."

LOADED

"I am pretty awesome," she laughed and put a hand to her belly, a subconscious gesture of every pregnant woman on the planet.

"Did you guys find anything helpful? We got eyes on a property where Farnsworth could be staying but these guys are good at being invisible."

Which meant I absolutely did *not* want to see whatever was on the flash drive.

"Come with me." I grabbed her hand in an overly familiar way that normally would have had me apologizing profusely, but now wasn't the time. I had to do this while I was too tired to think about it too much.

"Peaches trusts you and I trust her, so I'm going to trust you too, Vivi." I tugged her upstairs and into my room, closing the door behind us.

Her gaze narrowed. "With what?" The accusation was instantaneous, reminding me once again that I was an outsider, that no matter how Peaches felt, the rest of this crew saw me as an interloper.

"This." I shoved the red stick into her hand and took a step back, wrapping my arms around my midsection. "I knocked over one of the boxes on my desk and this fell out. It was inside a fake old fashioned tape recorder."

Vivi grinned. "I bought that for her as a gag gift about fifteen years ago." Her tone was wistful, and she shook her head in disbelief. "I can't believe she still has it."

"Anyway, I have no idea why it was in my office but I figured you'd know what to do with it, and you can pass the info along to Gunnar if it's anything worth knowing." I stepped around her and pulled open the door.

"Good luck."

She blinked and looked up. "I'm sorry, Anna—"

"Don't worry about it," I assured her. "You're worried about your friend. I hope that helps."

"I didn't mean anything by it," she said, sounding defeated.

"I know." And it did, it wasn't her fault that I'd fooled myself into thinking I belonged here. I'd never belonged anywhere, why would this ranch filled with veteran bikers and almost no women be any different?

"No harm done, Vivi. I just hope it helps us get her back."

"Me too," she said and left me alone. It was starting to feel like a theme in my life, one that I needed to learn to hate less than I currently did. I didn't need to belong on Hardtail Ranch because it wasn't my home. It was where a friend lived and where I provided some occasional medical assistance, nothing more. They weren't my tribe or my family, they were just people I knew.

Thinking of it that way was better. Smarter. Soon, Peaches would be back on the ranch with Maisie and Martha, and I'd be back at my house, alone, and life would return to normal.

Not soon enough.

Maybe when my life got back to whatever normal was, I'd make some changes. Go out more during my free time instead of staying at home and reading journal articles on new diseases and medical techniques. Maybe I would sign up for online dating—again—or maybe I would improve my vibrator collection. I could even take up a hobby.

A laugh escaped at the thought of that. I had almost no free time and the last thing I wanted to do when I had a few hours to myself was do more work. What I needed was a social circle. One that didn't revolve around this ranch, the club, or the bikers who lived here.

I stepped into the tub filled with hot, sudsy water and pulled out an emergency bottle of wine, taking an hour for myself before the guys headed back out and I was back on Maisie duty. I'd promised her a tea party, which meant I needed to stop thinking about all the ways I failed my patients today, all the ways I could fail Peaches if things went sideways, the big way I'd failed my father too. None of that mattered and I wouldn't let it interfere with my time with the little girl.

She deserved better than that, and I would make sure she got it.

Chapter Twenty-One

Wheeler

"Is Gunnar up here?"

I'd checked all the rooms on the first floor except for the kitchen. Martha shooed me out before I took two steps inside. "Got too much cooking today to be bothered by a handsome cowboy."

Me. She called *me* a handsome cowboy. I know what my face looks like and how women find it appealing, but the whole cowboy thing was kind of a hoot. Gave me a good reason to smile when everything else turned to shit, especially after the last few hours I'd spent on the phone.

Annabelle stared up at me, eyes slightly worried but trying hard to look normal for the sake of the little girl.

"No," she said, "I haven't seen Gunnar."

"Do you know where he might be?" She could be upset with me all she wanted, but now wasn't the time. "Don't make me ask you ten fucking questions, AB."

Maisie gasped. "You said a bad word."

"Adults don't always follow the same rules as kids," Annabelle told the little girl with a smile before turning back to me, where her smile died instantly. "I don't know where he is. He dropped Maisie with me an hour ago, and that was the last I saw of him."

"Thanks," I muttered but she'd already turned back to Maisie, my existence completely forgotten. I didn't have time now, but later, we had a few things to discuss. Gunnar had to be around here somewhere. Where else would he be?

The thought that he might do something stupid like go off on his own to take on Farnsworth had my feet moving quickly, back down the stairs and through the kitchen, ignoring Martha's cry. "There are two other doors in this house, boy!"

LOADED

There he was. Standing on the back porch, toes floating over the edge with his hands shoved in his pocket, looking like his mind was a thousand miles away. Then he said, "Please, God *fuck*, tell me you got something for me, Wheeler."

I stared at the back of his head. "How'd you know it was me?"

"Because even though Holden and Slayer are bigger fucks than you, nobody else walks like a two-ton beast. Must be 'cause of your leg?"

His casual mention of my leg threw me off, but I rolled with it. "Nah, my mom used to always compare me to a herd of elephants. Good thing the leg can handle it."

"Does it hurt?" His gaze never wavered from the horizon, lit up beautifully as the sun started her descent for the day.

"Most of the time."

Gunnar shot me a terse nod, and I stood beside him, both of us staring off in the distance, waiting for the next twist or turn in this strange conversation.

"Okay," he said, finally, his eyes still drilling the horizon. "I'm ready now. Whatcha got?"

"So I made some phone calls and got good intel. Looks like the death of your friend Bob Slauson ended the Gemini Program. He was the driving force and somehow found a way to make it work more often than it failed." It was a crazy ass story, and I was sad the world had lost Bob Slauson. "Must have been one hell of a dude."

"A chick, actually. She helped us with some shit back in Mayhem. Caused some too, but that's the nature of the biz, right?"

"Too right," I added with heavy shoulders. "Anyway the final Farnsworth, the one fucking with us now, has been AWOL since the op in Paris. I didn't get much info on the job just that the goal was achieved but it didn't go as planned. I got the feeling there's more to the story."

Finally, Gunnar turned his gaze to mine and cocked an eyebrow. "I was out here thinking the same damn thing. I let Peaches get away with being tight-lipped about this shit because after Vivi left to work for the Feds to pay off a Reckless Bastards debt, I couldn't risk that shit with Maisie, ya know?"

It had been me and Mitch for so long that I did know. "Yeah, but now you regret it. The same way I regret encouraging Mitch to become a head shrinker."

That pulled a snort-laugh from him. "Then Peaches came along, and I figured it was best to leave it behind us."

"You couldn't have known." The longer you're out of the military, the more distance you put between hard-learned lessons and your memories of them.

"I should have. Shit like this doesn't just die quietly in its bed of old age. We all know that."

He was right. "Okay but bitching about what you didn't do won't help us now. The agency, I assume it's the agency, but I could be wrong, has a crew searching for Farnsworth in Iran and Paris. I suggested they search a little closer to home."

"He's gone rogue," Gunnar said, fear lacing every syllable.

"Seems that way, but the good news is that the federal clean up crew still has an overnight flight before they're boots down in Texas, longer before they make their way to Opey." He blinked, trying to put all the pieces together. "We don't have any time to waste. If we don't beat them there, Peaches could become collateral damage."

Gunnar's eyes turned cold as he prepared himself for battle. All the emotion melted away except desire—desire to complete the fucking mission. "No fucking time to waste." He took a step toward the door before my words stopped him in his tracks.

"I'm coming with you."

"Fuck," he shook his head. "No, you're not. I need you here. With Maisie."

"Bullshit. You need me to be where I belong, at your side. When we get to that house, what are you gonna do if you find Peaches inside?" We both knew the answer but I needed him to see it for himself.

"I'll do what the fuck I have to in order to get my woman back. Her and our baby."

The fire in his eyes, that desperate mix of fear and rage was dangerous when it was uncontrolled like that. Wild.

"Exactly. And fuck the rest of us, right?" Gunnar was a fine leader, but he wouldn't be the first man blinded by love.

He frowned at me as his shoulders fell. "No. Of course not. But—"

"But your focus will be where it should, on your woman and your baby. This is what you have a fucking Veep for man. To be by your side and make the hard decisions when you can't."

I clapped him on the back to show that, with all the recent shit between us, I had his back.

"You lead us in there, and I'll back you up when you need me to." Our gazes locked for a few long, tense moments. His eyes searched mine and my face, in search of some truth he couldn't figure out. "I'm sober," I said to help him out. "No pills today other than some fucking useless ibuprofen. I swear."

"I trust you," he finally said. "I trust you Wheeler, otherwise I wouldn't have left Maisie's safety to you. That's why I need you here."

I didn't know what to say to that. It shocked the shit out of me to be honest. "Even after the leg and the pills?"

"I'm not thrilled you lied, but we all have secrets. Fucking secrets," he bit out with a growl. "I need to know Maisie is safe."

"She will be." Aspen's voice startled us both, and we turned to find her standing in the doorway with a double barrel shotgun resting at her hip. "We all love Maisie."

LOADED

Hazel was there too, looking too serious and fierce with a nine millimeter in both hands, a wicked smile on her face. "Can't leave a fellow troublemaker when she needs help."

And then Martha appeared. "I'll protect that little girl with my life," she added gravely. They all shared a look, and I knew that no matter what had happened between them, they loved the little girl equally. "Plus I've got Harold's Ruger," she held up a sturdy looking six-shooter with pride. "She'll be safe, I can promise you that."

Gunnar shook his head, overwhelmed by the women's gesture when Vivi stepped between them all and stood two feet from Gunnar, one hand on her hip and the other holding an AK. "She'll be safer than the rest of you motherfuckers, you can believe that."

"I can't let you get in the middle of this, Vivi." Gunnar wore a fierce expression that meant he would get his way, but Vivi surprised me. She notched her chin up high, looking bored.

"You can't stop me either. Leave a *man* behind if it'll make you feel better," she told him with a distinctive roll of her eyes that told him just what she thought of his idea. "But we've got this too, with our tiny female brains and all."

"Vivi," he groaned.

"Plus we've got the Doc here in case we need her," she said, rubbing her belly absently as she stared Gunnar down, daring him to waste more time. "Or we can keep bitching at each other while our girl is out there somewhere alone. Safety unknown."

That seemed to be the words he needed to hear to get his feet moving because Gunnar headed inside while I mouthed a heartfelt "Thank you," to Vivi as I followed behind him.

"Come on then, Wheeler. Get Ford to keep an eye on the…ranch," he said with one final look at the armed group of women, a smile ghosting the edges of his mouth. "Come on, we need to arm up."

LOADED

Those words put a smile on my face. Despite the shit storm brewing all around us and the danger of the night's mission, visiting the artillery room never got old. "You say the nicest things, Prez."

We both hopped on some waiting four wheelers and headed for The Barn Door and the Sin Room. And the removable wall that hid enough firepower to arm a small army.

Chapter Twenty-Two

Annabelle

"Dr. Annabelle, where's Peaches?" She looked up at me with big, worried eyes and it broke my heart. Maisie was no fool. She'd experienced enough loss in her life to know the signs that something was wrong. "No one is telling me anything 'cause I'm still a kid."

I remembered that feeling well, that feeling of hopelessness mixed with the knowledge that I wouldn't learn anything until it was too late. I let out a sigh and tried my best. "She had to take care of something, but she's coming back. Soon, I'd say." I hoped all that was true, because I didn't want to be remembered as another adult who had lied to her. Let her down.

"Promise?" In that moment I understood the fierce way Peaches loved this little girl and I envied the baby in her belly for having two parents ready with that kind of love.

"Yep, I do." My voice was overly bright, and I was sure the smile on my face teetered on the brink of wild woman, but I had to sell it. For a few more hours anyway. "Now, there are a lot of women downstairs who want to hang out with you. How does a grown up girls slumber party sound?"

When her smile lit up, I remembered how much I envied the joy and resilience of the young. Her face bloomed red with excitement. "Really? Can I stay up late?"

I gave her a gentle nod because I knew that no matter how things played out tonight, none of us would get much sleep. Except for Maisie. "Only if you promise to brush your teeth and put on your pajamas when I tell you to. Deal?" I held out my hand and waited.

Maisie looked at my face and then my hand, a small smile teasing the corners of her lips. She looked undecided, and I was totally smitten.

"You don't want to miss Martha's breakfast tomorrow, do you?"

LOADED

Finally, she put her hand in mine and gave it a solid shake for such a young kid. "Deal." She reached for her handy tiara, fixed it on her head and then marched out of her room and down the stairs.

I followed closely behind but not too close. We had a bunch of armed woman downstairs and even more firepower on standby. I wanted things to appear normal to Maisie, not look like she was walking into an armed militia. I heard the roar of a bunch of vehicles about an hour ago, a blend of motorcycles and a distinctive, bigger car. It would probably be a long time before we heard anything else, at least a few hours, maybe even days.

Luckily for me, Maisie was a super star among this particular circle of women. As soon as she stepped off the bottom stair, they engulfed her. Clearly in her element, she smiled and giggled as everyone made her the center of attention. She'd forgotten all about me, which made it easy to sneak off to the kitchen in search of coffee. As soon as I stepped inside the spacious room, my gaze lasered in on the half-full coffee pot, thankfully, still hot and steaming as I poured myself an oversized mug.

"Do you think she realizes she isn't alone?" That amused voice belonged to Vivi.

"Now she does," Aspen added, coming up behind her. She seemed even more amused.

I turned, mug still pressed to my lips and sighed. "Sorry. I didn't see you there."

"Clearly. Having dirty thoughts about the really beautiful one with the blue eyes?" Vivi arched a brow, mischief glowing around her like a halo.

"Wheeler? Absolutely not." Okay maybe that was too forceful a denial, but it was instinctive. "I mean, no. I was just thinking about how tense the air feels in there."

"Yeah, right," Vivi said, laughing shamelessly at my expense. "You believe her?"

Aspen shook her head, blonde hair spilling halfway down her back thanks to pregnancy hormones I could see blossoming on her skin, if she even realized she was pregnant yet. "Not even a little bit. I see the looks between you two. Give us something."

I didn't find sharing easy but I could speak about Wheeler now; it was over. "We have been sleeping together on and off for a few months, but it's off as of now."

"You gave that hunk up on purpose?" Vivi arched a brow. "I guess being a doctor does have its perks, like an endless supply of man candy."

I laughed and shook my head. "I was just a convenience thing. We were using each other, having fun and it was fine, until I went and developed feelings." Something I still couldn't admit without feeling foolish. "Damn daddy issues."

"Amen," Vivi said and raised her hand in the air.

"I hear ya, sister," Aspen added sadly, shaking her head. "We all have them. We just have to figure out how to deal with them. How to spot people that trigger our worst behaviors. It's just too bad for you that Wheeler has more baggage than your average fashionista."

That was an understatement if I ever heard one. "And he's fine with his baggage, happy to let it weigh him down." He would let it kill him rather than admit there was another way. A better way. "I'm done trying to change people, and I'm done changing myself to please people, and I'm okay with that decision." Or I would be, sometime soon.

Really, really soon.

"Or," Vivi added dramatically, "you could fight for him. Help him fight his demons. Fuck them out of him if that's what he needs. If you love him, that is." She shrugged like it was no big damn deal, like she hadn't just shattered my world with four simple words.

If you love him.

Did I love Wheeler? "No, I don't." I couldn't love him simply because I didn't know him. This was just a chemical reaction, an extreme side effect of really good sex. It wasn't the basis of a heart to heart connection or a long term, lifelong commitment.

"I don't," I said again, fighting against the way my heart leapt in my chest every time I even thought about the word. *Love.* I shook my head. I couldn't.

"Stand back, Aspen, she's figuring it out."

I ignored Vivi. She was wrong. Another classic case of a woman in love, with all of her dreams coming true, trying to make it so for everyone else. I didn't know Wheeler's middle name or his birthday or where he grew up. I couldn't tell you one detail about the scars on his body or even where he served in the military. I knew his blood type and his pain tolerance, things a doctor would know about her patient. You couldn't build a future on convenience. "I don't love him."

"Did you convince yourself already? Because we're totally not convinced." Aspen grinned cheekily, and I shook my head. "Men are stubborn, more so when their emotions are engaged. Holden hated me when we met because of a stupid comment I made when we were eighteen." My eyes rounded in surprise; Holden seemed to be the most even-keeled of the bunch. "I know! My point is that Wheeler gives off this vibe, that he's seen more, much worse than the rest of them. It's just hard to see because you're so blinded by his beauty."

I smiled at her casual mention of his looks, thinking how much Wheeler would hate that. Then my heart squeezed as another thought came to me. These two women seemed to know him better than I did, and Vivi had only been around a few days. *Because that's how Wheeler wants it.* "I appreciate your insight, really I do. But I'm tired of not being enough. I can do that on my own."

Vivi let out a snort-laugh that was as out of place as it was funny. "Oh please. You're a doctor, and you're pretty, if a little nerdy. You should be too much for most men. When you believe it, they will."

Her words resonated with me the longer I sat with them. Between those words and worrying about Peaches, my mind was full. I was grateful to the rest of the women for lavishing attention on Maisie. After dinner she brushed her teeth and put on her pajamas without a fight, but only because Hazel promised to braid her hair. She enjoyed her night, only vaguely aware of the danger the two most important people in her life were in at the moment.

I worried enough for the both of us, probably enough for every woman in the room. I couldn't help it. Because I knew the real life damage guns did, fighting did, weapons and war did. I couldn't help it because I cared about these guys. I might be an outsider, an interloper who pushed her way inside, but I gave damn and not just about Wheeler. About all of them. They were gruff and rough and a little too damn tough, but they were good guys. Nice guys.

They were—all of them—good men.

And I hoped they all made it back safe and sound.

KB WINTERS

Chapter Twenty-Three

Wheeler

We arrived at Early Healey's property just after sundown, all of us scattered around the edges so we had views on all angles. Thankfully, Healey's land was flat and open so even from a quarter mile way, we had eyes on the inside. The place had been abandoned for a while according to the fading paint and dilapidated porch, but I was thankful only three windows had shades; the rest were bare.

Gunnar crept closer, eager for news off Peaches. "It's just like Big Mac said," I told him. "Two figures inside. One armed."

"That has to fucking be them," Gunnar insisted right in my face. "Who the hell else could it be?"

He was right, of course. "We can't just go in there guns blazing. This dude has some serious training. What if the place is rigged? Booby trapped?"

His shoulders fell, and he started to pace. Again. "Fine."

"Cruz, we got ears on yet?" Another reason it had taken so damn long to get out of the artillery room was that Vivi and Cruz spent thirty minutes huddled in a corner, talking tech.

"Thirty seconds," he responded short and sharp, too focused on the task at hand to give a fuck about niceties. "Okay. Tune to channel seven."

Seconds later, the crackle of channel seven gave way to voices. One very familiar, the other not so much. "Just tell me where the flash drive is," That came from a male voice, deep and nondescript. Farnsworth.

The next voice was unmistakably Peaches. "I don't know what you're talking about. What flash drive? Can you describe it?" Even over transmission, Peaches did a shit job at pretending innocence.

The sound came loud and sharp, flesh against flesh. "Answer me and this can go a lot easier."

LOADED

"Oh, now I know what you're talking about. Nope, no I don't." You could hear the smile in her voice, even when things weren't looking good for her.

"A fucking firecracker, like I told you." Gunnar knew but he needed to hear the words. He flashed a reluctant grin until we heard another slap.

"I can do this all day *Peaches*. Can you?"

She barked a laugh that had as much pain as bravado in it. "I don't have to do it all day, just until my guys get here."

"You could be dead by then." His voice came out cold, matter of fact, and we all knew it wasn't a ploy.

"I could, and if that's the case, whatever you're looking for dies with me." Her logic was impeccable but listening to this, knowing how unstable this guy was, made it difficult.

"Let's go inside." Gunnar was getting antsy but until we knew exactly what Farnsworth was looking for, this shit might never end.

"One more minute," I warned. "We have to end this Gunnar."

Farnsworth laughed. It sounded low and deep and half-crazed. "Who said it would be over? I might have to kill your whole family until I find what I'm looking for. Gunnar. Maisie. That doctor friend of yours. She's real cute. Perfectly corruptible." He smacked his hands together loudly. "All the rest of them until I find what I need."

"And you still won't find it. Tell me what this is about, and maybe I can help you out, Farnsworth."

He smacked his lips together. "Oh you really are as smart as everyone says you are. It's why I wanted you on the Paris job in the first place. It's why it'll be such a loss for the Agency." I didn't believe the fake sympathy or some other attempt at emotion in his tone.

The sound of the gun cocking had us all advancing forward, and then a gunshot ripped through the air. Every last one of his stood stock still, holding our breath as we waited for a sign that Peaches was still alive. "You crazy motherfucker are you trying to make me deaf?"

Collectively, our shoulders relaxed, and we crept forward until we could see the details on the other side of the window.

"Just tell me what I want to know. Where is that fucking flash drive?"

"Like I'd tell you even if I knew after that bullshit stunt. Goddamn, that was loud!"

Farnsworth stood abruptly and knocked over the rickety old chair he'd been sitting on, turning over a side table that had seen better days. "I know you have it. No one else does."

Peaches laughed again, and Gunnar and I shared a look, knowing that answer wouldn't go over well with a guy like Farnsworth.

"Or maybe, just maybe, they're very good at hiding secrets." I could hear the contempt in Peaches" voice. "You're not the only one good at lying. All of you have a very important tell."

"Lies!" Farnsworth's hand landed on her cheek again, the sound deafening in the dark silence. "You know this doesn't end until I'm satisfied."

Cruz snickered in my ear. "Sounds like something you'd say to every woman you ever sexually disappointed."

"I'm going in. Now." Gunnar's chest heaved and his nostrils flared. I had a second, maybe two, before the Prez went rogue.

I gave Gunnar a nod, our gazes locked to make sure he didn't do anything reckless. "Slayer, lights on my signal." Darkness wouldn't provide that much cover for a man with Farnsworth's training, but it would give us enough of a lead to beat this fucker.

"Waiting on you, pretty boy."

"Fucker," I growled and motioned for each man to move, and Slayer signaled to the man on his other side until we were all advancing on the raggedy-looking cabin.

"Now, Slayer."

LOADED

A moment later the lights inside went out and we breached from all available entry points. Gunnar went straight to Peaches, using his big body to cover hers as bullets went flying throughout the house. I cleared a path to the front door so Gunnar could get Peaches out, shooting off a couple rounds to disorient Farnsworth.

"Take her!" Gunnar shouted the words at me and I shook my head. This was his rescue, and he should be the one to get her to safety.

"This is all you, man."

"No, I need to make sure this fucker is gone. For good this time." He cracked his knuckles and flexed his fingers, stretching his neck muscles in the universal sign for *I'm ready to fuck someone up*.

There was no arguing with him, and since Peaches was safe, I had no right to get in the middle of this fight. "I got her."

"Not yet you don't!" Farnsworth took a big swing at Slayer, knocking him down, before aiming his gun at us, releasing two rounds. "You're mine."

I couldn't say for sure how I knew, only that I had a gut instinct that this guy wasn't just unstable, but also reckless.

"Stay down," I shouted to Peaches and shoved her out the door, following her until a bullet sliced across my thigh and sent me face first to the ground.

"Fucker!" I turned and aimed my weapon, getting two bullets off before Slayer and then Gunnar blocked my view.

"Come on, dummy. You can't help them if you're hurt.." Peaches grunted and tried to pull my arm.

"You think you can pull more than two hundred pounds of muscle, and I'm the dummy?"

"Just shut up," she growled and helped me stumble away as blood poured down my leg.

"You all right? Other than a few smacks, I mean?"

She beamed a smile up at me. "You worried about me, Wheeler?"

LOADED

"We all are." With a big tree for cover, I dropped down on my ass and leaned against the wide trunk, sucking in air and trying to ignore the pain roaring through my body.

"Next time I get kidnapped, I'll remember that." Her nose wrinkled at the sight of the blood running down my leg. "That doesn't look so hot."

"Have a seat. You look like you're about to fall over." Bullets still flew inside, but then, moments later it felt silent.

Peaches took a seat beside me and patted my leg, using it to propel her body against the tree. "I could use some water. And all the food in the world."

"It's over!" Farnsworth's voice echoed around the flat land around the Healey Ranch and then two shots rang out, and no one said anything for a long goddamn time.

"Now it's over," I moaned and let my eyes fall closed.

"Um, what is this?" Her hand slipped at the sound of the gunfire and found my prosthetic leg.

"Guess you've been gone longer than I realized. I have a fake leg. Lost mine in the desert."

"Damn. Really?" I nodded and wrapped a strip of fabric around my thigh to stop the bleeding. "How did we not know that?"

"Didn't want you to, I guess." That was the damn truth, but it turned out that hiding it was worse than their reactions could have possibly ben.

"Annabelle knows."

"Hard to hide when you're fucking." My voice was gruff and those words unnecessary, but she was the last person I wanted to talk about at the moment. "I don't want to talk about AB."

"AB, huh? Sounds like it's more than fucking."

Yeah it would sound that way to a woman. "Just focus on your own babies, Peaches."

"Thanks to you boys, that's exactly what I plan to do."

"Good," I grunted.

"That doesn't mean I won't find a way to repay you. All of you." Her words were vague but filled with mischief.

A sudden commotion interrupted the peace. A ratty old van with different color painted panels came to a dust-kicking start about twenty feet from where Peaches and I sat. Gunnar and Cruz dragged Saint while Slayer took up the rear, the raggedy group heading our way.

"What the fuck happened?" I asked, wincing with pain.

Gunnar grinned, his lip split and bloody and one eye starting to bruise. "This shit is over. All the fucking way over. Finally." His gaze went directly to Peaches and the smile they shared was intimate, too damn intimate. I tried—several times—to stand and put some space between us.

"You got some lead too?" Saint wore a lopsided smile and clutched his side while Gunnar and Peaches wrapped around each other and kissed like they'd been apart for decades.

"Yep. Just a flesh wound though."

"Same here. I call shotgun on having the Doc fix me up. Your time with her might take…longer."

"Asshole," I grunted while Slayer continued to laugh.

"Mitch?" I said, not believing my brother stepping out of that van to rescue us. "What the hell are you doing here?"

"I'm ambulance transport. Get your bloody ass in the van. You too," he barked at Slayer. "Anyone else?"

Gunnar shook his head, eyes never leaving Peaches. "Thanks, Mitch."

"Don't mention it."

LOADED

Cruz helped me into the van and slid in after Saint, shaking his head. "Brother you've got learn how to dodge bullets, or you'll look like a voodoo doll."

Saint rolled his eyes. "Very funny. And what did you do?"

"I put one of the two final shots into that motherfucker. I only wish I had more fucking bullets."

"Amen, brother." Mitch slammed his foot on the gas and we took off down the dirt road, leaving the others who weren't hurt to deal with the bikes and bodies.

It was time to head back to the ranch.

Chapter Twenty-Four

Annabelle

"Do you need anything for the pain?" Standing beside Wheeler like nothing was wrong—because nothing *was* wrong—I summoned all of my medical training and employed deep breathing techniques. He'd been shot. An actual bullet had ripped through his flesh on their mission to rescue Peaches.

Which they had. Thankfully.

But still, seeing Wheeler shot had hit me like a ton of bricks. It affected me in ways I couldn't possibly have anticipated. Which was ridiculous. The man spent years in the Middle East on missions he couldn't talk about even if he was the emotionally available sort of man to talk about his feelings. With someone. Hell, with anyone.

He turned to look at me over his shoulder, one dark brow arched in my direction. "You seriously asking me that?"

Under normal circumstances, I would have agreed that it was a ridiculous question, but these were not normal circumstances. "You've been shot, Wheeler."

He snorted. "It's a flesh wound, AB."

If he could dismiss his pain so easily, so could I. Mostly. "If the pain worsens double up the ibuprofen."

"And if I need something stronger?"

I knew what he was asking, at least I thought I did. I shrugged as though it didn't matter. "Then ask your brother. He can write you a prescription." I finished bandaging his leg, making sure a thick layer of disinfectant covered the wound, trying to touch his bare skin as little as possible. I might be upset with Wheeler, but I wasn't immune to his appeal. Not yet.

"That's cold-blooded, Doc." He shook his head in my direction, a tiny smile curving his lips into a tease.

"Sometimes that's how a girl's gotta be. You're good to go." I took a step back and then another until I could suck in a damn breath without inhaling his scent.

It was dirt and sweat and man, mixed with leather and something else. Whatever it was, it was too potent and with my heightened emotions in that moment, I needed distance.

"So I'm dismissed?"

"Your wound is bandaged, Wheeler, end of story." I wasn't in the mood to fight. "Let me know if you need anything else." The men had returned to the ranch about an hour ago, a little beat up with a few wounds that I needed to clean and stitch up. Martha stared at us impatiently, waiting for someone to clean up the medical exam room so she could have her kitchen back.

"I need to talk to you." His gaze bored into mine, sober and serious. His deep blue eyes were as clear as I'd ever seen them.

"Not now." Martha hovered close by, the stove sizzling and bubbling as all kinds of aromas filled the air. She was cooking for the men like they were heroes returning home from the war. I guess they were, in a way, because though the Reckless Bastards returned with just a few injuries, that haunted look in their eyes said they'd done things they'd left the military to avoid.

"Soon," he insisted and I gave a short nod of agreement even though I had no plans to have any kind of talk with him.

"Go put some heat on those muscles but make sure you don't get the bandages wet," I reminded him with a small smile, sorry to see another scar marring his gorgeous body.

"Yes ma'am." He flashed a boyish smile and gave me a salute before sitting up and sliding off the table. I watched him go until he was out of sight, enjoying the view of his ass and thighs in well worn denim.

"I sure wish you two would quit skirting around each other and just make it work already." Martha grumbled more to herself than to me as she wiped down the table, sending gauze and cotton swabs and tape flying to the floor.

"Leave it, I got it," she insisted when I bent to pick up the debris.

LOADED

"I'm just trying to help, Martha."

"You've helped plenty, stitching up those boys without getting the police involved. You're a good woman, Dr. Keyes."

'Thank you, Martha. You're pretty damn good yourself." Even with the haunted look in her eyes, the look I'd seen on many women who'd lost a child, she defended Gunnar and Maisie, this house, and the club with her every breath. "Are you sure I can't help?"

The older woman nodded her gray head in the direction of the doorway that led to the rest of the house, where Peaches hovered nervously. "You can put that one out of her misery. She's been waiting with the patience of a hungry feline."

I laughed and went to Peaches, wrapping her in my arms for the first time since she walked through the door in Gunnar's arms. I was happy to see her unharmed other than a few bruises and a split lip. "So happy to have you back."

She squeezed me so tight I groan before she pulled back with her signature throaty laugh. "It's so damn good to be back! I didn't think Maisie would ever let me go."

"Did my best to take care of the little rascal and shield her from as much of the danger as I could, but she was pretty worried about you."

"Me too," she said and rubbed her belly. "Told me you took excellent care of her. I even heard something about a tea party."

That small gesture reminded me of the parts of her life she kept from me. I didn't know about their little chat. "It was nice. Do you want me to take care of those," I asked pointing at the wounds on her face.

"That would be great. Let's go upstairs so we can talk." Before I could tell her I wasn't in the mood, she grabbed my hand and tugged me up the stairs and down the hall until she was sitting on the edge of the tub in the master bathroom. "I can't stop smiling."

LOADED

"The shock is wearing off," I told her and worked silently but efficiently as she told me the details of her kidnapping. I barely listened because it wasn't something I wanted to think about. More to the point, I didn't want to have to figure out how to *stop* thinking about it for the rest of my life. So, I listened with half an ear while I disinfected cuts, stitched her lip, and applied bandages. "I'm gonna check your vitals to make sure you and the baby are fine." I took several deep breaths and took her blood pressure. "BP and pulse elevated but normal considering everything. You should take it easy over the next couple days and then go see your OB, okay?"

She nodded. "Are we good?"

"Yep, we're great. Now that you're back. I'm more upset with myself that I didn't notice you were so far along." Her clothes weren't particularly baggy, but in hindsight, she'd been wearing a lot more tunics and flowing *hippie shirts* as Martha called them.

"Almost seven months. I've been trying to hide it, I was so afraid that if I even spoke about it, somehow they'd find out. I told Gunnar to keep quiet as well."

I nodded, understanding. Peaches was still a friend. Just because we didn't share every part of our lives, didn't diminish her importance in mine. "Now that's not an issue, we'll have to hurry to get a baby shower planned." I flashed the best smile I was capable of in the moment.

But she still stared at me, like she was searching for something. "Are *you* okay?"

"Me? I'm fine. Nothing to worry about." I put a final butterfly bandage on her cheek and stepped away. "And you are too. Better?"

"Yeah. Exhausted and achy. Hungry as hell." Her smile belied her words, and I knew she was happy to be back with her family. "And you?"

"Fine. Ready to sleep for a few days," I assured her.

LOADED

"Sounds like a good idea to me. Vivi has to get home before she has those babies in the air, so tomorrow I plan to sleep like the dead." Peaches stood and wrapped me in another hug and this time I leaned into her and accepted the affection. Holding her tight and maybe a little longer than necessary.

"I'm so damn glad you're all right, Peaches. Both of you." I said as I rubbed the baby bump. How had I not noticed?

"Thank you for keeping my girl safe. You're the best."

"It was my pleasure. I want you to eat and then rest tonight and all day tomorrow. Listen to your body."

"I will. Thanks, Annabelle."

"No problem," I said and repacked my bag, ready to head back to my home and my bed. "Call if you need anything."

"You're leaving?" I didn't miss the flash of disappointment in her eyes, but I needed to get back to my life.

"You guys should enjoy some time alone. Together." With a final wave, I turned away and walked down the familiar staircase as the kitchen exploded with the sounds of conversation and laughing. I wanted to go in there, to belong to this rag tag group of people who fought hard, played hard, and loved just as hard.

But I didn't feel like I belonged there. They weren't my people; they belonged to Peaches. And Wheeler.

I took one last look at them, the men hugging and kissing on their women, laughing now that the danger had passed.

Then I walked out the front door and didn't look back.

Chapter Twenty-Five

Wheeler

Peaches was back at home on the ranch where she belonged. Both mother and baby were safe. I was pretty sure Gunnar would keep them both wrapped in cotton for the next hundred years or so. I popped a couple ibuprofen because no matter what Annabelle thought, I was done with that other shit. Completely and totally done with stupid fucking pills that didn't dull any of pain, only made me an asshole to the few people who gave a shit about me.

And I was hauling ass toward the big house because it was a little past noon and Martha had promised another feast now that all the trouble had passed. And because I couldn't wait to tell Annabelle…a lot. We had a lot of things to discuss and top of that list was an apology. For using her and for being such an asshole for no good damn reason. I saw the expression on her face last night. She was worried. About me.

Annabelle was a beautiful, accomplished woman, sexy and intelligent, and *she* wanted me. For whatever crazy twist of fate the gods were playing at, Annabelle wanted me. A banged up old Ranger with enough baggage to fit on a luxury jet and a bum leg to boot, and she wanted me.

It was damn time I stepped up to be the man she deserved. If she would even give me a second chance. Or was it the third? The fifth? Whatever chance it was, I would grovel if I had to.

The main house was chaos. Absolutely fucking chaos in the best possible way. Even Holden had dragged his ass away from his woman and out of that little cabin long enough to join the rest of us to make it a full house. Gunnar held Peaches close while Maisie talked her ear off about whatever it was that fascinated little girls. Saint and Hazel sat near the other end of the table, quiet and lost in each other. Slayer and Cruz joked around while Mitch kept mostly to himself, always on the outside looking in.

We were alike in that way.

"Well, well. The hero has finally decided to bestow his presence upon us!" Slayer stood and bowed with a flourish, both middle fingers aimed in my direction along with a luminescent smile.

"Yeah and *fuck* you too." I mouthed the word.

"Wheelie, you saved Peaches!" Maisie scooted off the bench and ran over to me, slamming her little body into mine and hugging me fiercely. "Thank you, Wheelie."

Even the cutesy nickname was beyond sweet so I ignored the guys laughing and bent down to scoop her up. "It was my pleasure. She's my favorite smart ass."

Maisie gasped. "You said a bad word."

"I did? No I didn't, I said she was an intelligent donkey." With the most innocent look I could muster, I stared into her blue eyes until laughter shook her little body.

"No, you didn't!" The sound of her giggles bounced off the walls, bringing a smile to every mouth in the room. Kids had a way of making people forget all the hell they walked through and just feel happy that they did it to get to this one moment. Another quick hug, and I was forgotten about in favor of another round of chocolate pecan pancakes.

The seat across from Saint was empty so I grabbed a mug and took that seat. Martha wouldn't suffer anyone trying to take over her kitchen, even if it meant something as simple as getting my own coffee. "Smells real good, Martha."

"Tastes even better," she called out confidently and I nodded my agreement. Despite the drama with her daughter helping a club enemy, Martha didn't seem to hold a grudge, which only made me respect her more. Losing a child was never easy, but it was smart of her and the other twin to stick around. They were safe here.

I had no doubt about the quality of the food, so I dug in, grabbing one plate just for a stack of plain buttermilk pancakes drenched in butter and syrup and filled the other with biscuits, bacon, sausage, eggs and hash browns, while casting clandestine glances around the table. It was a man's breakfast, and I was starving. None of us had been able to eat much before taking on Farnsworth. Martha's late night meal had been like an appetizer. I'd gotten up early and rushed over here from the bunkhouse for two reasons, breakfast and Annabelle.

Breakfast was delicious and slowly disappearing.

But where was Annabelle?

"She went home last night," Cruz answered a question I hadn't asked, not out loud anyway.

"Who?"

"Who, he says." Cruz smacked Slayer's arm and laughed, giving him a 'can you believe this guy' look while pointing at me. "The pretty little doctor, that's who. She's gone."

Dammit. It had been a mistake to assume she'd stay once the trouble had passed. The club had turned her life upside down, at least for a few days, and she was probably eager to get back to normal. Whatever that looked like for her, because I never bothered to learn. "Hmph," I grunted in reply.

"Eloquent," Slayer laughed and shook his head. "Let me give you a tip about women, Wheeler. They like it when you at least *pretend* to like them." He shrugged. "I find it helpful, and I'm irresistible."

Cruz laughed. "You wish, man. That whole mountain man look is played. The ladies are all about the exotic look these days."

"Doesn't matter what you look like if you act like an asshole, though. Am I right Peaches?" Slayer asked.

She blinked and stared at Slayer before nodding back at me. "Language, and yes. Even your pretty face can't overcome being an asshole, Wheeler. Care to fill me in?"

I shoved a final pancake into my mouth and stood. "Hell no, not even a little bit. But I am glad you're okay," I told her and went to smack a kiss against her cheek. "Gotta go."

LOADED

"She's not as tough as she looks." Peaches whispered the words in my ear and looked deep into my eyes to make sure I understood.

I did, but she was wrong. "You're right, she's a hell of a lot tougher." She just didn't know it yet.

Peaches nodded, a small smile gracing the corners of her mouth. "Good luck. Annabelle is stubborn and reluctant to trust."

I barked out a laugh at that understatement. "No kidding. Take it easy today, or I'll tattle on you."

She gasped in outrage, and I gave her a playful wink before leaving the main house, leaving the Reckless Bastards and Hardtail Ranch in my rearview while I went in search of AB.

I knew she wasn't at home the second I pulled up. The windows were all dark and her car was nowhere to be found, but still I climbed the stairs and knocked. And waited.

Two minutes later I was back on my bike and headed for the hospital. Suddenly, it was important as hell that I see Annabelle now, that we clear the air between us. Last night I'd done plenty of thinking before drifting off to sleep, and my thoughts were full of one person, one thing.

Annabelle.

The crazy damn woman was already at work after nearly a week of drama and danger, not to mention looking after a kid during that time. And instead of resting or having a spa day like rich lady doctors tend to do, she was back at work. Healing the sick and bandaging the injured. And when I stepped inside the chaos of the ER, I found her kneeling in front of an old man who was trying to look down her shirt.

"I'm pretty sure trying to get a shot of cleavage is a clear sign this isn't an emergency, Elmer." There was clear amusement in her voice, and the old man smiled even as a dangerously red flush stained his cheeks.

"No harm in trying to do whatever I can to feel better, is there?" He shrugged and flashed another grin. "I don't mean no harm, Doc."

While he talked and flirted, she laughed and joined in, taking notes one minute and checking his pulse the next. "I know you don't, old man. I just have to keep you on your toes, maybe then you'll start taking care of yourself."

"And give up our little dates? How could I?"

She was gorgeous as she tilted her head back and laughed. The sound was as beautiful as it was welcoming, soft and feminine but also sultry and smoky. "You're good for my ego, too, Elmer. No more barbecue this weekend, okay?"

"But Doc, the football—"

She held up a hand, her serious doctor expression stopping whatever excuse he'd been about to offer up. "No excuses, Elmer. Your blood pressure is too high. Next time you come in here like this, I'm admitting you."

He stood and glared at Annabelle and I flexed my hands just in case she needed me. "What the hell kind of Texan watches football without a damn barbecue?" he grumbled

He continued to whine, and I was grateful only for the fact that it kept her laughing.

"The kind who wants to see if the Cowboys ever make it to another Superbowl?" she said.

More than half the waiting room groaned at her dig, and she laughed even harder. "Try chicken breast. Or cauliflower. I hear its all the rage these days."

"I understand the rage part of that, Doc. You have yourself a good weekend, and I guess I'll be having chicken."

She laughed again and patted his back. "You'll be perfect. I'm even rooting for the home team," she assured him and guided him toward the door.

"That was pretty damn impressive."

She startled and turned with a wide-eyed gasp at my words. "Wheeler? What are you doing here?" Immediately her shock turned to worry. "Is something wrong? Is Peaches all right?" Hand to her chest, Annabelle was a picture of concern.

It gave me the perfect opportunity to get my hands on her, even it they did just rest on her delicate shoulders that felt far too frail lately. "Everyone is fine. Eating too much and talking way too loud. I came to check on you."

"Me? Why? I'm fine." She tried to step back, away from my touch, but I couldn't let her. Not yet.

"I needed to see for myself you were fine. You left before we could talk."

Her expression softened slightly. "Did you sleep well?"

This was exactly why I was here. Annabelle was good people, through and through. She gave a damn about other people, even when she shouldn't. "Dreamless and peaceful. Nothing but that damn ibuprofen too."

Surprise showed, but she banked it quickly and looked around. I did too, noticing that we had a pretty big audience of nosy townspeople and even nosier nursing staff.

"I'm glad to hear that, Wheeler. You look well rested, but how is your pain?"

I shrugged. "Better than it should be considering what I put my leg through yesterday, but I can manage it. I promise." She opened her mouth and I cut her off, smiling. "I'm taking it easy *and* listening to my body."

Finally, I earned a smile just for me. "I guess I tend to sound like a broken record to my patients. Hazard of the job." She shrugged it off and tried to step around me. "What are you doing?"

"We haven't talked yet."

She sighed and went around me, slapping a folder on the large round reception desk in the center of the room before turning back to me. "In case you haven't noticed, I'm at work. Some place I haven't been all week because I've been busy with *other* things."

"Which is why I'm here, AB. To make sure you're not exhausted. To see if you need lunch or maybe a ride home after work?" Yeah, I sounded like a sorry ass pussy whipped half man and I knew it. The strange thing was, I didn't give a damn. Not even about the young nurses clearly lingering behind Annabelle for the sole purpose of eavesdropping.

"Thank you for the offer, Wheeler, but like I said, I'm fine."

"You're damn stubborn too." She was so determined to be strong, to show the world just how strong and independent she was that the frustrating woman didn't realize when someone was offering a hand.

"Then why are you here?"

"Because I can't stay away, AB."

She barked out a laugh. "You've managed just fine over the past few months. It might take some time, but I'm confident that with a little effort you'll be able to again."

I blinked in surprise at her words and looked around the room to see if there were hidden cameras around. "You want me to stay away?'

A throat cleared and we both turned to the woman behind the desk. "Maybe you two want to take this conversation somewhere more private? Get some privacy, at least."

"Right." Annabelle nodded and flashed a grateful smile at the woman. "Thanks Tish." She motioned for me to join her, and I followed her down a long hall, shaking my head at the way her baggy work attire hid all those sinful curves. The ones that had haunted my dreams all last night.

"This is a little too private, don't you think?" The elevator was too small, it made me far too aware of the petite brunette beside me. Even through the stench of hospital disinfectant, I could smell her scent. Her essence. It had me leaning in closer to her, hungry for any part of her.

"We're going to the cafeteria. You can talk while I grab some breakfast."

LOADED

I didn't bother telling her that it was late afternoon and far past the breakfast hour because I didn't think she'd appreciate it. "You're buying me a meal? This is already going better than I expected."

I ignored her glare. "Did you hit your head last night?"

"No," I sighed and stepped off the elevator first, holding the door for her. "But I've been acting like an asshole for no reason, and I'm sorry AB. You didn't deserve it. Any of it."

She froze and turned to me; eyes narrowed to suspicious slits. "Really?"

"Yeah, really. Is that so hard to believe?"

"Kind of, actually." She grabbed a tray and picked up a salad and a burger. "I appreciate the apology, but it really isn't necessary, Wheeler."

"Because there's nothing between us anymore?"

She swallowed, but in her hesitation, I had my answer. She was already pulling back, I could feel it. And didn't it just make me the world's biggest asshole that the feel of her pulling back only made me want her more? No, not more, but it made me realize how *much* I wanted her. How much the thought of not getting to see her again, up close and in my arms, actually affected me.

"Was there ever?" she said. "Besides sex, I mean?"

Fair question. But dammit, why couldn't she just listen to what I was saying in the moment? "Maybe not but just because there wasn't doesn't mean there can't be. Right?" I scratched my head and rolled my eyes. "Did that even make sense?"

AB found a table easily since there were only a handful of people in the cafeteria, choosing a table with a view of the outside. She dropped down and carefully laid out her silverware and then placed the napkin over her lap, covering the blue scrubs she wore.

"You want us to be friends?"

"Among other things, yes. Is that so hard to believe?"

LOADED

"Honestly, Wheeler, it is. I tried to get to know you all these months, without any ulterior motive. I just wanted to know the man I was sharing my body with. You didn't want that, and you made it abundantly clear."

"And things can't change? I'm just a broken down, pill popping solider, right? Once a thing, always a thing. Is that it?"

She shrugged and spoke around her hamburger. "Your words not mine."

"Bullshit."

"I admire your service even though you're determined to forget it ever happened. I don't give a damn about your leg. It means you paid a heavy price to help keep this nation safe, damn you. I don't think you're even a pill popper. I just think it's easier to take a pill rather than, I don't know, maybe *fix* your problems." She took another bite, this one angry and forceful, leaving me speechless. "Nothing to say? I'm not surprised."

"Why is that?"

"Because you never, ever have anything to say Wheeler. It's kind of your thing, the quiet, brooding, bad boy. I thought it was just an act, now I'm not so sure."

Dammit, I was losing her. Again. If I ever had her in the first damn place. She was uninterested at best and putting more distance between us with every passing moment.

"Isn't that part of the appeal?"

She snorted. "Hardly."

Ouch. "So it was just the sex, then?"

"Wheeler, I'm not doing this with you. Not today. Not now." She shook her head, smiling knowingly at me. "I don't think you really want me, Wheeler. I don't even think you like me all that much, so really, what is this all about?"

"I want you AB. I want to get to know you, what makes you laugh and cry. What else makes you horny.

Why you don't talk about your parents. Why you came to Opey. I want to know it all."

"That sounds nice," she started, and my shoulders relaxed. "But why should I believe you?"

Damn, Peaches was right. AB didn't trust easily. Maybe not at all. "Because I'm saying the words to you. To your face. Right now." I leaned forward on my elbows until just a few inches separated us. "That way when I start to show you the truth, you'll know why." When I pulled back, AB looked bewildered. Completely shocked by my words.

"You...what. Why? No." It wasn't coherent or positive, but strangely I wasn't worried.

"I mean it. Because you're kind of incredible, AB. A chance, that's all I'm asking for." It was all I needed.

"A chance." She whispered the words and closed her eyes, almost as if she was trying to envision what it might look like, giving me a second chance. Was she wondering if I'd show up for sex and then leave before the condom hit the trash can?

"I don't know, Wheeler."

"That's the point, AB. I fucked up, and we both know it. But we're never gonna know if we're good together if we don't try, right? That's pretty much the scientific method."

Her serious expression melted and a small laugh escaped. "Is it? Then how can I—"

The nurse from earlier approached our table with an apologetic smile. "Dr. Keyes, I just got a call from Darryl, a bull broke free over at the county fair. At least a dozen injuries coming our way, including two cowboys with hoof marks where there shouldn't be none." She caught her breath and flashed a shrug my way before shuffling away.

"Damn." For a moment, AB looked stricken, and I realized she dealt with the same trauma I did, only it was all day every day, Nonstop. "I have to...go."

"Do what you have to do. We'll talk again, AB. Soon."

She nodded and stood, letting down her long brown hair and retying it into a ponytail and pushing those sexy red glasses back up her nose. "At least I got to finish most of my breakfast. Look, Wheeler, I appreciate your sentiment, and I admit, I'm tempted. But I just can't. I need to make better decisions."

"And I'm a bad decision?"

She nodded. "No, that's not right. I don't regret it, but we don't even see eye to eye on casual sex. Surely you can see how complicated anything else might be."

"Complicated is my thing. I'm not afraid. Are you?" Before she could come up with a smart ass answer, I brushed a gentle kiss to her lips and walked away. This wasn't over yet. In fact, I was just getting started.

Chapter Twenty-Six

Annabelle

"You have a good evenin', Doc." Tish called out her farewell with half of her body already inside the passenger seat of her car as she waved at me. "Enjoy having a day off. You've earned it!"

I sighed and sent a tired wave to Tish and her family. "Thanks. Enjoy your day of shopping."

"Oh I plan to, honey. Good night!"

It was hard not to smile around Tish, even at the end of a twelve-hour shift that had turned into a fifteen-hour shift thanks to a texting teenager. Exhaustion wore on me, heavier by the second as I slid into my own car and aimed my wheels towards the familiar path home. My mind wandered all over the place, at everything and somehow also at nothing. My thoughts swung wildly from the kid I couldn't save today to Wheeler's words.

To the man himself. True to his word, for the past five or six months he'd been putting forth a full frontal assault to *show* me that he gave a damn. Whether it was the cutest text messages telling me little details about him, like his favorite color, blue. Or his favorite meal, fried chicken with mashed potatoes, gravy, and sweet peas. His favorite movie, *Forrest Gump,* but he tells people it's *Born on the Fourth of July.* He'd been making a real effort since brushing that kiss across my mouth in the hospital cafeteria and walking away with his lazy, leggy gait and, I was sure, a satisfied smile on his face.

I still didn't trust his motives or how long they would last, but it was kind of nice to have someone so eager to talk to me and hear what I have to say. Even if nothing came of it, or if something did but it didn't last, I promised myself that I would enjoy this. Getting to know a man like Wheeler, so masculine and strong but somehow vulnerable and broken too. It was a compelling mix that beckoned me closer when a smarter woman would be running as fast as her legs would carry her.

"And there he is." My headlights illuminated his big, masculine form, reclined on a on the steps of my porch, relaxed as all get out with his long legs spread across nearly every step. Every so often he would show up like this, to chat and sometimes more. In the few months since the shootout, I'd almost become used it, though not quite.

I sucked in a deep breath and took in the sight Wheeler made in his dark jeans, bunched around the ankles thanks to his big black leather motorcycle boots. The light gray shirt he wore over his leather vest should have been plain, basic even, but it made him look like every cowboy fantasy I'd ever entertained. And he was on my porch.

Waiting. For me.

With that thought, I took a deep breath and let it out as I pushed open the door of my car and stepped out into the cool night air, letting the soft breeze cool my suddenly overheated skin.

"Wheeler," I grunted despite the way I stood straight up, taking notice of him. "What are you doing here?"

"Tempting you," he said with a smile and pushed off the steps until he stood in front of me, tall and imposing with his sexy smile.

"With?" As great as sex with Wheeler was, I was tired to even entertain that thought right now. Mostly, even if my nipples disagreed at the moment.

"Dinner. Made by these hands." He showed off both sides of his large, slightly scarred hands before picking up two paper bags I hadn't noticed until now. "What do you say?"

I gave a short nod. I was too tired to fight and wasn't dumb enough to turn down a home cooked meal made by a handsome man. Yeah, okay, and maybe there was the tiny little fact that I hadn't been able to stop thinking about Wheeler's words, especially the *kind of incredible* part. No one had ever called me incredible before. Bright and smart, sure. Articulate, without a doubt. Pretty sometimes too, but never incredible.

Hell, I wasn't sure anyone had ever even thought I was incredible. and it was kind of...exhilarating. To know that this big, strong, capable man thought I was incredible.

"All right come on in," I told him after a long, drawn out silence.

He flashed a boyish smile that made my knees weak and put his hand on the small of my back, guiding me inside my own home. "I hope you like steak."

"I'm a Texas girl," I told him, utterly offended. "Of course I like steak."

"Good," he grinned again and this time it was darker, with more intent. "Because I can do excellent things with meat."

I stared at his too-handsome face for a long moment before I burst out laughing. "I'm sure you can," I told him on a laugh. "A skill I'm sure comes in very handy at The Barn Door."

He quirked a brow at me, and I laughed again, suddenly feeling light and young and carefree, an odd thing to feel after fifteen hours of blood, guts and death. "I'll give you that one for free."

The heat in his eyes distracted me for a moment, giving Wheeler plenty of time to invade my space, to press his big body against mine until goosebumps broke out on my skin and produced a shiver. Then he leaned in, and before I could think better of it, his lips were on mine. Soft and firm and demanding absolute and total submission. I submitted, because what the hell else could I do when his lips and his tongue glided against mine, harder and harder until I vibrated with need, inching closer because it wasn't enough.

Nothing was.

Eventually, we broke apart naturally, smiling at each other with giddy, matching grins. "Never gets old," he growled and kissed me again. This time it was soft, gentle even, and then he stepped back. "Better get going or it'll be midnight by the time we eat."

LOADED

Midnight wasn't too far off and there was a good chance we'd sit down for dinner about twenty minutes before a new day began. "As long as I can eat it, after I get cleaned up, I don't care if its breakfast."

His lips curled into an affectionate grin I couldn't ignore if I wanted to so I nodded, hiding my nervousness behind a laugh. "Good to know. Bad day at work?"

The concern, genuine concern, in his deep blue eyes affected me in ways I didn't even understand. I nodded. "Let's just say it wasn't good. A hot shower and a stiff drink, and I'll be as good as new." I didn't have to be at the hospital tomorrow so I might even have two stiff drinks.

Wheeler groaned. "Let's not talk about you naked and in the shower. Not yet."

"Naked is generally how people shower, Wheeler." His lips pursed and his jaw clenched, like he was trying really hard to be good. It was a pity really, but since I was covered in dried bodily fluids and probably a few visible spots too, I decided a shower was my main priority. "Music is on the window ledge and booze is in the cabinet. Good luck and try not to burn down my kitchen."

He laughed. "Oh ye of little faith. You'll be eating those words right along with my juicy meat."

The thought of his meat had me shivering, and I hurried to put some distance between us before I did something silly like beg him to toss me on the counter and make me come at least twice. Maybe more, if he was up to it. Hell, if *I* was up to it. Instead of responding, I slowly climbed the steps and made a beeline to the master bath that had a soaking tub and a glassed in double shower. It was why I'd bought the place and why I refused to get a bigger space.

I took my time in the hot shower, letting the hard spray beat the tension from my muscles until, slowly, I began to feel normal again. As normal as I could after the day, the week, even the month I've had. The hot spray beat down my back and over my head, and I let the recent events of my life replay in my mind. Sewing up bullet holes and cuts, treating bruises and abrasions. All that was in addition to my work at the hospital, fixing broken bones, defective organs or parts mangled by motor vehicles. I had to wonder, when the hell did *this* become my life?

When did I keep company with bikers? When did I have friends period, never mind the kind who kept big, life altering secrets from me? When did I start letting strange men into my home to take over my kitchen? This life wasn't what I pictured, not even a little bit, when I was a little girl trying hard to impress my father. But as I stepped from the shower and dried off, taking my time drying my hair and rubbing moisturizer all over my body, I realized I was happy with my lot in life.

Mostly.

Would I love to have a man look at me the way Gunnar looks at Peaches? Absolutely, but my life isn't suffering because I don't. I have a job I love and I happen to be very good at it. I have a great home with an amazing shower, a growing group of friends that could *almost* be classified as a support system. I had nothing to be down about or ashamed of, and I wasn't.

This wasn't the life I'd mapped out with the eyes and thoughts of a little girl, but it was the life created by a woman who knew life didn't always turn out how I thought it would. It was a good life and right now, it featured a sexy as hell motorcycle-riding veteran with a bad attitude and a body made for sin.

And I was upstairs, lost in my thoughts. Squandering the moment.

I got my head screwed on straight and fifteen minutes later I was dressed for comfort, not to impress, and headed back towards the kitchen. "Smells like more than steak in here." It smelled divine, like peppers and garlic and cumin. My stomach growled at the aroma and I was grateful for the rock drifting from the wireless speakers.

"That's because it's steak tacos." He smiled, looking so proud, and I felt myself being pulled in to his orbit, into the world where he ruled over all.

"I even made salsa." He nodded towards the table where a big bowl of salsa sat beside a platter of chips. "And I toasted the chips."

I turned to him and arched a brow. "Careful, Wheeler, I might start getting ideas."

He grinned. "That's what I have in mind, AB."

There it was again, those eyes and the nickname and the playful smile that actually made me *start* getting ideas. Damn him.

"Well let's see if the chips and salsa impress." I felt Wheeler's blue eyes on me as I drew closer to the table and picked up a warm chip before running it through the salsa.

"Damn," I said after a savory bite, "that is impressive. And spicy," I told him with a smile.

"You ain't seen nothing yet, AB."

***

"You make a damn good margarita, AB." Wheeler smiled at me from across the sofa where we relaxed with a pitcher of margaritas on the coffee table beside the platter of chips and salsa. Talking. Again. Getting to know each other, with our clothes on.

"Should I be offended at your surprise?"

He grinned that *aw shucks* grin that I was sure had all the old ladies in town pinching his cheeks and longing to pinch his ass. "Not offended. You're a regular Renaissance woman."

I laughed. "Good save." Talking to Wheeler was nice. When he wasn't being a surly ass who hid every emotion behind a steel wall, he was actually charming. And funny. And so damn sexy, I needed to make this my last margarita or we'd be naked before he had a chance to mash up the guacamole. "So, why steak tacos?"

"You love steak and I love tacos." His words were simple but they meant so much to me.

"I do love a good piece of thick, juicy meat." I was playing with fire, I knew that, but a gorgeous man had kicked off his shoes and made food to nourish me from scratch, I was allowed to act a little bit slutty, right?

"Annabelle," he groaned and dropped his head between his arms. "You're killing me."

"By talking about steak?" I blinked slowly, feigning innocence, enjoying toying with him. Just a little.

"AB," he said, his voice a warning.

"I thought guys loved talking about steak. There's so many cuts of meat. Thick. Thick and juicy. Big. Big and juicy. So juicy that it makes a mess. Everywhere." Okay, maybe that was pushing it a little. I blamed exhaustion and margaritas, and the calming presence of Wheeler.

"Annabelle," he growled and the sound of my name on his lips, send a visible shiver through me that he not only noticed, but decided to pounce on immediately. Wheeler slid across the sofa until our bodies touched. It was an innocent touch, his knee and thigh pressed up against mine, but the intent in his eyes wasn't innocent. Not at all.

"You're playing with fire."

Yes, I was playing with fire and I knew it, but the margaritas were making me feel a little bit reckless. I was overdue. "Maybe so, but it's a controlled burn. Right?"

Though Wheeler was fully capable of losing himself in the midst of carnal pleasure, I knew I didn't have to worry about him getting lost in anything more significant than that. Even if I was slowly starting to wonder myself.

Wheeler's serious expression morphed into a dark smile. He leaned in with a nod. "It can be controlled, but when it comes to you babe, all bets are off."

I wanted a second, just a moment to let those words and the way he said them sink in, but his lips were on mine in an instant. They were firm and commanding, perfectly at home taking charge of the kiss, directing my movements like a skilled maestro. His mouth devoured mine and his tongue played and teased until I vibrated and purred like a kitten in his arms.

I couldn't get enough of this man, and it was damn disturbing, a thought that, no matter how fast or frequently it came, I couldn't quell the heat simmering inside of me. Every swipe of his tongue was another bolt of lightning darting through my body, leaving streaks of white heat imprinted on my skin. His hands roamed and wandered, adding to the heat already making my skin boil. "Wheeler," I moaned when his tongue skated along my collarbone. "Please."

A primal grunt sounded at my words and he deepened the kiss, pulling me onto his lap so our bodies were perfectly aligned and holding me close, like he couldn't bear for me to be too far away from him. "AB, I can't resist you."

"Who's asking you to?" I cupped his face with a smile and leaned in, softly brushing my lips against him, laughing when he held me tighter, closer and, growling into my mouth hungrily. We kissed like that for what felt like hours and hours, getting lost in the taste and feel of each other.

Wheeler stood with me in his arms and I let my body slide down the length of his, hitting every hard ridge and plain on the way down. He groaned and took my mouth again, hungry and intense this time as he stripped me out of my clothes.

"AB," he said in a sexy hiss when I was fully naked I stood there and let him absorb every detail. "Fuck me, you get more gorgeous every time I see you."

His words pleased me, and I stood a little taller, sticking my chest out and enjoying the way his gaze centered on my breasts and the puckered nipples punctuating them.

"I'm right here, Wheeler. What are you gonna do about it?"

He smiled and took a step forward, putting one hand on my waist and pulling me forward. "You."

LOADED

His mouth was on mine and this time we didn't stop. Our lips never parted as we kissed and kissed. All over. Everywhere. I was naked. Wheeler was naked, and we stared at each other for several long, tense moments.

Then, he pounced.

Wheeler was on top of me, half on and half off the sofa, one hand sliding up my thigh while the other palmed my breast, my hands found their way to his cock, long and thick and pulsing with need. "Please," I begged and gave his thick cock a squeeze. He growled and bucked his hips until his cock surged into me, filling me up deliciously.

"Yes!" Just what I wanted.

His lips curled into a tight smile and then his hips were moving, fast and deep, and with an intensity that hadn't existed between us before. He was beautiful, glorious to watch with his handsome face twisted in erotic agony. I couldn't look away as he pumped into me, pelvis against pelvis, drawing my orgasm closer to the surface.

"AB," he growled, gripping my hips and thrusting harder, faster, deeper into my body.

It felt so good I wasn't sure if I could take any more pleasure, but oh God, how I wanted it. His body, so slick and hard in my hands, vibrating with the pent up tension of his restraint. "Wheeler."

"AB," he whispered back, moving faster and faster into me, pulling pleasure from me a little at a time until I was close to begging for the orgasm that was just out of reach. "Ah, Annabelle."

I closed my eyes at the soft-spoken way he said my name through gritted teeth and arched into him, trying like hell to block out the emotions that were trying to work their way to the surface.

"Oh yes, Wheeler!" Then it was a sweet explosion of colors and fireworks as pleasure coursed through my veins and filled me completely. "Yes!" The words fell from my mouth like a prayer and I couldn't stop, not even as he thrust hard and faster through my orgasm, jump starting another one just as the first one died down.

"AB, oh fuck!" His hips bucked wildly and his hands gripped me so hard I knew there would be bruises later but I didn't give a damn. Pleasure oozed out of my pores and my veins, maybe even my hair follicles. His big body collapsed against mine was the only thing keeping me from spinning off the surface of the earth and right into the outer space.

"Fuck. AB." His words came out on harsh breaths that made me smile. It was nice to see that Wheeler could be so deeply affected.

"You just did that." I laughed at the offended look he wore and pulled him down for another kiss. "And it was fantastic."

"Fantastic, huh?" He grinned and flexed his hips before collapsing once more and rolling to the back of the sofa and pulling me close. "I can't think of a better word, so you win."

I laughed again and turned to face him, resting my face over his racing heart and my hand low on his belly. "I feel like a winner."

"Yeah?" He wore a goofy smile and I nodded, sure my own smile was as goofy as his. "That's my line, babe."

Babe. That word from his lips brought a smile to my face. I don't think anyone had ever called me babe, at least not in *that* way. "Well I took it, so you have to get a new one." And then because I was feeling sexy and like a 'babe' who was in charge of her pleasure, her sexuality and her choices, I turned to Wheeler and took what I wanted.

Again and again.

Chapter Twenty-Seven

Wheeler

"It's all right if you have to go, Wheeler." AB's voice came out small but sure behind me as I sat up, rubbing my leg. My aching leg.

I didn't move, but I didn't say anything either, letting her words linger in the air to see if she wanted me to go or if she just assumed I would. Again. "I'm right where I want to be."

She sighed and fell to the bed, rolling around until her legs were tangled up in the sheets. "Okay," she said simply, though she couldn't hide her surprise for shit. "Suit yourself."

I smiled, knowing she couldn't see me. She was so damn tough and independent, it was going to be hard to break through her walls. "I think I will, if you don't mind." After two rounds of sex and more steak tacos than two people should legally be allowed to eat, even in Texas, we finally made it to the bedroom.

She gasped when I slid between the sheets and pulled her body flush against mine. "When was the last time you slept with someone?" It wasn't something I particularly wanted to talk about, but this was part of getting to know her, right?

Annabelle thought about it, as was her way, and let out a long breath. "Seventeen months."

My eyes bugged out. "You've gone seventeen months without sex?"

"I didn't say that," she said with a laugh, turning in my arms so we were face to face. I smacked her ass for being so coy and the moan she let out hit me straight in the cock.

"Okay, smart ass, what side of the bed do you prefer?" I never bothered to stick around long after sex so it wasn't information I needed. Ever. But I guess in the spirit of healing and all that shit, it was time to move out of the bunkhouse. Maybe get my own place or share a place with Mitch since it looked like he planned to stick around for a while.

"Wherever I generally fall asleep. Depends on if I'm reading or watching Tv. Or masturbating." She flashed a saucy grin at my obvious distress and pressed her body against mine.

"Don't say that, AB. I'm trying to get to know you, dammit." The woman would kill me before I found out anything significant.

She sighed and laid her head on my chest again, something I was growing more addicted to by the second. Her soft hair brushed against my skin as she got comfortable.

"Okay Wheeler. Get to know me some more."

All week I'd been playing a childish game of twenty questions in an effort to learn more about AB. Peaches hadn't been much help, refusing to answer anything and insisting I ask the woman what I wanted to know. And I had. "Kids?"

"Yes, eventually. Two, maybe three. You?"

That was easy, and I should have expected it because AB wasn't like most women. She didn't start planning the wedding on the first date, probably waited until the hundredth date. "Maybe. I haven't really thought about it much since losing my leg."

Annabelle's stare turned serious and she sat up, those big brown eyes focused solely on me as she cupped my face and forced my gaze to hers. "I can attest, personally and professionally, that everything works fine. You're young and healthy," she said on a frustrated sigh. "Don't be stupid, Wheeler. If you want kids, that," she pointed at my leg, "is no reason *not* to have them."

Her words shocked me, but not more than the vehemence behind them, like she really believed that. Like she didn't think it was crazy for a one legged man to want to have a kid.

"My staunch defender now, AB?" It was a nice feeling, to have someone other than my unit or the Reckless Bastards looking after me. Defending me.

"I like you, Wheeler." Her words were simple and heartfelt, with no ulterior motive I could discern. "When you're not being an insufferable asshole, that is." Her smile took the sting out of her words, which we both knew to be true.

How in the hell was a man meant to concentrate when those feather soft fingertips brushed over my skin, specifically the tattoo on the right side of my chest. "And even if you *are* an asshole, maybe you won't be an asshole to your kids. You have loyalty and integrity, and I think you might have a few other good traits to pass along to a kid or two."

Her words shocked the hell out of me. I'd stopped thinking about kids or even a serious relationship. I wasn't interested in the hassle of a woman getting used to my leg or learning to live with it. I had no desire to be anyone's compromise, dammit. "You think that?"

"Damn right I do." She nodded firmly and flashed a bittersweet smile I didn't understand. "My dad. My parents, they had everything and I didn't want for a thing that could be bought or rented."

"Must be nice," I added with a snort, wondering if I had anything to offer a woman who came from so much.

"You'd think so, but I didn't get much of their time or guidance, and no benefit of their intelligence other than genetically. Instead I grew up awkward and reserved, especially compared to my successful parents. In case you haven't noticed."

Her little pout was sexy as hell and cute, but I valued my extremities too much to risk telling her that.

"Oh I noticed," I told her and leaned in to kiss the strip of flesh between her neck and shoulder, where one little freckle rested all on its own. "And it turns me on. A lot," I told her and kissed the same strip of skin on the other side of her body. "In case *you* haven't noticed."

She laughed and traced a finger along the stubble at my jaw. "You fogged up my glasses so believe me, I noticed."

I shrugged. "So, maybe I have a thing for doctor girls in glasses."

"Doctor girls?" She arched a grow, looking even more like a sexy teacher or a naughty librarian, even with the mussed hair. Even without the glasses.

"Yeah, you got a problem with it?"

She thought about it for a second and smiled, shaking her head. "Nope. I kind of like it, I think."

That shit was music to my ears. "Good, because I'm thinking about buying a pair or two, just for the bedroom."

She laughed. "So this thing about nerdy girls, it's a full on fetish?"

I nodded. "It's a very specific fetish."

"How specific?" The question rolled off her tongue on a teasing purr that had my cock waking up from his hours long slumber.

"Annabelle specific," I growled and stole a kiss that she quickly melted into, tangling one hand in my hair and the other on my ass.

"Good answer," she purred and sat up to straddle my hips. Her brown eyes stared deep into mind and from this distance, I could see the threads of gold that illuminated every emotion she felt. "So you were serious, about us, I mean?"

"Hell, yes," I told her firmly. "I know my mind, AB."

She nodded, acknowledging the truth of my words with a respect that made me think I could really love this woman. If I didn't fuck it up first. Slowly her mouth pulled into an affectionate grin. "Okay, then. I'm in." She smiled and leaned in to flick a tongue over my nipple.

"Ah, AB."

"I am so, so in," she purred and then spent more time than I ever allowed a woman to spend with her mouth on my body. Pleasing me. Exploring me.

Driving me mad with desire.

Chapter Twenty-Eight

Annabelle

The feeling of the sun splashed across my face gently tugged me into consciousness, pulling me from a deep, satisfying sleep. My body ached all over, deliciously so and a smile touched my lips as I arched my back and stretched my muscles until they screamed. The ache brought back the memories of last night, the endless pleasure and the sounds. *Good God, the sounds!*

Last night had been different than I imagined it would be. When I pulled into my driveway to find Wheeler on my porch, I expected an edible meal and a few quick orgasms before he disappeared into the night. I couldn't have imagined the delicious meal he'd whipped up from scratch with his very large, very calloused and very capable hands. Or the way he held me tenderly and kissed me like I meant something to him.

Of course that thought was quickly doused like icy water when I turned, still smiling, to find the other side of the bed empty. Not just regular, the other person is in the bathroom empty, but ice cold. Wheeler was gone and he had been gone for a while. Typical.

I let out a sigh and sat up, scanning the room for any sign that I was overreacting and that Wheeler hadn't, once again, taken off like a fucking thief in the night. I wasn't and in a way it was comforting. Last night, hell ever since Wheeler called me incredible, I'd been wrestling with my feelings and trying to get my emotions under control. Now though, it looked like I worried for nothing. Wheeler hadn't meant any of his words and I wasn't special to him. I was another Saturday night lover.

Nothing more.

With that depressing thought, I got out of bed and stopped in the bathroom to wash my face and brush my teeth, the way I started every morning. Thankfully, it was still fairly early. I had no place to be today, which meant I could take my time getting through the day.

LOADED

Grabbing my robe on the way out, I wrapped it around me and made my way downstairs and headed towards the kitchen. The living room was empty save for my discarded clothes strewn about the room all alone, looking like the world's saddest party had taken place.

Coffee. I needed coffee. It was the only thing I needed first thing in the morning. Not Wheeler. Not any man. No matter how disappointed I was to see him gone.

Or...not gone because there he was, in my kitchen. Cooking breakfast. Shirtless underneath the blue and white heart printed apron, arms bunching deliciously with every move he made. I watched him for several long minutes, soaking up his masculine beauty and the graceful way he moved around my kitchen. He looked up at me, feeling my stare on him, and grinned. "Mornin'."

God that smile was a panty soaker. It was damn near irresistible and when combined with that apron and those muscles, well my pussy clenched and leaked just as my body woke up and took note of all the details I could see above the counter.

"Wheeler," I breathed, still not quite able to believe he was here. Still here. "Good morning."

He grinned but there was a serious glint in his eyes. "Thought I booked it again?" He arched those chestnut brows at me, lips curled slightly in amusement. He wasn't offended, not at all, but more curious than anything.

"Yes," I told him honestly. "I'm glad to see you didn't." So glad that I didn't want to think too hard about why my chest felt lighter. Freer. "Coffee?"

Wheeler grinned and granted me the out I was seeking with a nod, before he turned to the coffee pot and poured two cups. Still rooted to my spot near the kitchen table, I watched him move and wondered about his uneven gait.

"Here ya go." His blue gaze was on fire as his tore through me, taking in every inch of skin he could see behind the short silky robe I wore. Then he leaned across the counter with a smile. Waiting.

I couldn't resist this man at all and definitely not when he held a cup of piping hot coffee for me in his hands so I leaned across the counter until my feet were airborne and pressed a soft kiss to his cheek. "Thank you."

"You're welcome," he growled, but before I could pull back, Wheeler's hand speared through my hair and held me close while his tongue plundered my mouth, exploring every nook and crevice with his tongue until I was soaking wet between my thighs, weak-kneed and ready for my next orgasm. "That's better," he said and pulled back, putting some distance between us before I could protest. "Cream and sugar are on the table."

Damn this man for affecting me the way he did and damn my stupid hormones for making me too attracted to him. Too damn addicted to the things he did to my body. Too intrigued by the way I responded to him, in and out of bed.

"You cooked breakfast," I said inanely as I dumped too much sugar and cream in my coffee.

"I did." He flashed a proud, boyish smile. "I was bit of a shit in my early days in the Army. Did more than my fair share of kitchen duty, believe me." He smiled again and I had to have an internal talk with my body and my heart, to stop with all the noise. Even if I did tell him that I was in, I wasn't ready to be *this* in. Not yet.

"Smells good." The table was already half full of food, yet Wheeler was still behind the counter, flipping something on the stove. There were sliced strawberries in a bowl beside a big plate of scrambled eggs with onions, bell peppers and cheese. Bacon and hash brown cakes rounded out what was on the table. I was stunned. "You didn't have to do all this, Wheeler." It made me uneasy as much as it made me feel special, to have him doing so much. It felt like he was trying too hard.

"I know." His gaze held mine, and he flipped the last pancake onto a plate, still not looking down, and made his way to the table.

I gasped when I caught sight of Wheeler and the reason for his uneven gait. "Wheeler," I whispered, touched and emotional and uncomfortable as hell. His prosthetic leg was nowhere to be seen. Instead he wore a crutch that wrapped around his forearm. "Wheeler."

He flashed another of those lazy grins that was somehow teasing and sexy. "I planned to have this off and do a big reveal while we were eating, but I guess I didn't knock you out as thoroughly as I anticipated."

His words knocked me down into a chair. He'd planned this out prior to this morning. What in the hell did that mean? "It's the coffee. It wakes me up every morning ten minutes before my alarm sounds."

"Good to know. Next time I'll have to love you better than coffee." His blue eyes seared through me, and I tried to block out the *love* word he used, because *of course* he didn't mean he would love me. It was my body we were talking about. Nothing more.

"So this is me," he began with a nervous smile, motioning towards his missing limb once he got rid of the plate. "Scars and missing leg and all, this is me AB. I'm damaged, fucked up beyond repair probably, and I'm not comfortable with it. Not as much as I should be. But I'll get there."

He was being honest and sharing, and it was scary to hear these heartfelt words from this man. Big and strong, and stubborn as hell, Wheeler wasn't the guy who cut himself open so you could see him bleed. Yet here he was. Bleeding. For me. "I'm not asking you to change, Wheeler."

"I know, but I want to be the kind of man you deserve. No, I want to be *the man* you deserve. Me and not some other fucking man."

I smiled at the energy in his voice. "You already are." The words slipped out accidentally. They were true, absolutely true, but I hadn't meant to blurt it out so easily. So carelessly.

He shook his head and raked a hand through his hair. "I'm not. Not yet and not by a long fucking shot.

But I want to be, so fucking bad, and I will become that man. I'm just asking for a little patience, AB."

Patience. It was easy to ask for, but could I really stick around and hope for the best where this man was concerned? Would I be waiting for years before he realized he needed professional help? Thankfully before I could say a word in response, the phone rang. No, two phones rang. I made it to both phones first, tossing Wheeler his as I answered my own. "This is Dr. Keyes."

"Annabelle, it's Gunnar. The baby is coming."

"Now? It's too early." She still had over two months to go before her due date but sometimes babies showed up early, and with the shit Peaches had been through, I just prayed the baby was all right.

"Yes, already, Annabelle. We need you." Those words had my feet moving quicker than anything else would have.

"I'm on my way. Where are you?"

"About to leave for the hospital as soon as Cruz gets his ass over here to watch Maisie. Will you be there?" The fear in his voice startled me.

"Yes. I'll meet you there. I promise."

"Great," he said and ended the call.

I turned and found Wheeler staring at me.

"Peaches is having her baby. We need to go now." The arrival of a baby was always a good thing and this one would be met with a ranch full of love.

"I guess we'll pick this up later?"

My heart squeezed at his words, so softly spoken and filled with such vulnerability I nearly cried. "I'm not looking for perfection, Wheeler. And even though your face comes pretty damn close, that's not real." I smiled at his confused frown and rubbed the pad of my thumb along his jaw line. "If you want to become better, that's what I want for you. And I hope I'm around to get to see it. Now let's go."

He took my wrist and turned it over, pressing a hot kiss to the pulsing throb there. Then he pressed another kiss further up my arm and another, further still. "Anytime you want to see it AB, just say the word."

He smiled and leaned in, and I smiled and stepped closer, putting one hand over his heart, feeling the way it thundered under my palm. Then we were kissing one another. It wasn't a slow, sensual kiss. This kiss was full of fire, white hot and quickly boiling out of control. I clung to Wheeler and he held me close, kissing me until I was breathless and his cock, long and hard, pressed against my belly. "Wow."

"That's a word I never get tired of hearing from your sweet lips." Just to punctuate his words, he leaned in for another kiss that was slow and sensual, almost spiritual as it went on and on and on. "We'll pick this, and the conversation up again. Later."

I gave a short nod and watched as he walked away, barely noticing anything but his shirtless back until he disappeared from view.

My heart raced and my mouth ran dry as butterflies took flight inside my belly, and I knew I was in deep, deep shit.

Why? Because over the months of slowly getting to know him, he'd worked some magic on me.

And I was in love with Wheeler Haynes.

Chapter Twenty-Nine

Wheeler

"Holy shit man, you're a dad." I clapped Gunnar on the back, wearing a mile high smile that matched his own. "A daddy."

He glared at me, and I laughed. "Don't ever call me daddy. Ever."

"How is she?" AB had rushed back to the maternity ward almost as soon as we came to a stop in the hospital parking lot, and I hadn't seen her since.

"Holding up," he answered with a worried shrug, his gaze still on the double doors that led to the maternity ward. "Doesn't want me in there, if you can believe it. Said she wants me to want to visit her down there again one day soon."

I barked out a laugh. "Sounds exactly like some crazy shit your girl would say," I told him with a disbelieving shake of my head.

"Right?" Gunnar shook his head, affection evident in his expression. "What the hell is taking so long though? All the fucking books say first babies come quick."

Slayer snickered. "Maybe your kid, but mine will never come quick."

Gunnar flipped him off and we all laughed just as the double doors burst open and AB appeared, wearing one of those ugly blue shower cap things over her thick brown hair and her street clothes had been replaced with scrubs. She smiled at Gunnar and wrapped him in an uncharacteristic hug. "There's an adorable little boy back there I think you'll want to meet. He's early. Little guy, but healthy as a horse."

Gunnar blinked and nodded, his feet rooted to the floor until I clapped him on the back. "Come on, bro. I'll go with you to meet your kid."

Gunnar swallowed and nodded his appreciation as we followed AB back. "A boy. Shit man, I've got a son." Happiness rolled off the Prez, and I couldn't help but smile, thinking that Peaches had been kidnapped and held at gunpoint not long ago, and now they were happy and welcoming a new life to the family.

"We already have one girl to worry about, plus all the women." It was enough to make sure the MC never got a moment of rest, constantly worrying about keeping little girls safe. "A boy is good. One of us."

His lips tipped into a grin and I shoved him into the room where Peaches sat up in bed, looking beautiful and exhausted. And happy. "Hey, babe."

She smiled prettily and rolled her eyes. "Hey yourself. Come on over and meet our little boy." Gunnar walked to her on shaky feet and AB took his place beside me as we watched the emotional moment in silence. "Hey, Stone, this is your daddy, Gunnar. He's big and strong, and he's gonna take care of you."

Gunnar looked like he might cry as she handed him the baby, smiling awkwardly when AB moved in to help. "He's so small."

Peaches snorted. "Five pounds, three ounces is hardly small, at least not for my lady parts. And even if he came early, he's healthy."

"TMI," I told her, making her laugh.

Gunnar looked at me and grinned. "A fuckin' son, man!" His deep voice startled the baby, and a cry tore through the air, making Gunnar jump. "Shit, what did I do?"

Peaches laughed and shook her head, holding her hands out to take Stone from his dad. "Didn't you do all this just a few years ago with Maisie?"

"She wasn't this small, or maybe she didn't seem so small," he stuttered, looking bewildered by the tiny crying baby he couldn't take his eyes off. "He's got my eyes."

"He does," Peaches said sweetly. "And my crazy hair."

At her words I took a step closer and smiled. Sure as shit, this little boy, Stone Gunnar Nilsson, was a perfect blend of his parents. He had Peaches' copper curls on his head, pale brown skin, and Gunnar's deep blue eyes giving the boy a shocking and adorable appearance. "Cute."

"Cute? He is fucking adorable," Peaches insisted and dropped a kiss on his forehead. "Aren't you?"

"Of course he is," AB cooed, looking over Peaches' shoulder with a wistful smile.

"Glad you think so," Peaches said with a smile. "Because Gunnar and I want to ask you and Wheeler to be Stone's godparents."

I froze and looked to my Prez. "You sure about this man?" I knew that the secrets, the pills and my leg had dented his trust in me, and I hadn't earned this responsibility. This fucking honor.

"Absolutely. You're the only one who doesn't trust you yet." With those words he waited for my answer.

"Yes. Abso-fucking-lutely, man." We shook hands and hugged it out the way men do, before he turned his attention where it belonged. On his family.

"Come on, let's give them some privacy and share the news." AB tugged on my hand until we were out of the room and walking down the fluorescent-lit halls, the sounds of the hospital swirling around us.

We passed a small closed-in patio area, and I tugged on her hand to make her stop until she looked up at me, a question in her eyes. "It's time."

AB's shoulders relaxed and she nodded, falling into step beside me. "I suppose it is."

Her words were resigned, which I didn't understand, but I would. We walked into the green lush area surrounded by colorful flowers and trees and instantly all the tension in my shoulders fled. Between two pots of roses, we sat on a bench with a gold plate commemorating the life of a beloved woman, and I took her hand in mine. "AB."

"Wheeler." She smiled but it was sad. Again, I didn't understand.

"Are you having doubts?"

"Constantly," she said on a laugh. "But I meant what I told you last night, I'm willing to give us a try."

It wasn't a ringing endorsement or even a sign this was something *she* wanted, leaving me more confused than ever. "AB, I'm terrified too. What if you wake up one day and realize you can do so much better than a damaged vet with a bad attitude?"

She nodded and squeezed my hand. "And what if you wake up and decide you want something more than a boring old nerdy doctor who spends most evenings reading medical journals?"

I frowned at her. "Hey, that's my woman you're talking about." That pulled a smile across her face, and she was more beautiful than ever.

"Your woman, huh?"

I nodded. "If that's what you want, it's sure as hell what I want. You, AB, you are what I want." My heart raced as the words came out of my mouth, faster than I could edit them. "We're as different as night and day on the surface, but you were right. I never let you get to know me and I did everything I could to avoid getting to know you. I regret that now."

"I don't."

"You don't?"

She shook her head and removed that ugly ass cap so her hair fell around her shoulders, thick and beautiful so that I wanted to run my fingers through it. Soon. "No. I'm glad I got to know the real you when you wanted me to. I hate practiced flirting and charming."

I smiled, knowing Slayer's skills with the ladies would never have worked on a woman like AB. "Good to know."

"I don't want to spend our time together regretting the past, Wheeler."

Her words caught me off guard. "Does that mean we'll have more time together in the future?"

She nodded. "As long as you keep trying, and I keep trying, then I don't see why not."

I appreciated that she thought it might be so simple, but I wasn't as sure. "AB," I sighed.

"No. You said you wanted to be better and you can be. You will be. Because of you, not me." She turned to me and cupped my face. "While I love that you want to be someone you think I deserve, I think that you deserve to be the man you were before you lost your leg. Hell, I think you deserve to be the man you'll become. I'll bet Mitch does too. And Gunnar." She pressed a soft kiss against my mouth. "My guess is you're the only one who doesn't see that."

"Ah, shit AB." This was what made it all so hard. She was fucking irresistible. "This is why I love you. Your ability to see me as something more than the man I've shown myself to be. It's humbling. It makes me want to earn that look in your pretty brown eyes."

"L-L-Love?"

I nodded, barely holding in a laugh. "Is that a surprise to you?"

She nodded again. "Uh, yeah. Pretty big surprise, actually."

"Unwelcome?" I held my breath as I waited for her to answer.

Thankfully, it came quick. "Not at all. I'm still scared as hell of giving you my heart, but it does help." She smiled, and I relaxed but only slightly.

"Help with what?"

AB sighed and let her thumbs graze the length of my jawline, back and forth, in a soothing motion that calmed my racing heart. A little. "Knowing you love me makes it a little less scary that I'm in love with you too."

"You're...?" My mouth or maybe it was my brain, one of those fuckers lost all ability to think straight, to form words. I just nodded. And nodded as a stupid ass grin spread across my face. "Say it again," I insisted, making her laugh.

"I said," she said and stood between my legs as she looked me in the eyes. "That I am in love with you, too." She stared at me as the words sank in, an unstoppable smile lighting up her face. "How do you feel about that?"

"Like I'm the luckiest bastard that ever lived." I hoped that one day she might grow to love me and might get used to loving a man with only one leg, but today? It didn't seem real. "You sure? 'Cause this leg ain't growin' back, babe"

She laughed and nodded. "I'm sure, but I might have to reconsider if you think there was ever a possibility that leg could grow back." Her lips touched mine in a whisper of a kiss. I held her close, deepening the kiss to make sure this was all true. That she was really mine.

"AB," I groaned, and she wrapped her arms around me and held me close.

"Wheeler. Stop giving me an out when I'm not looking for one. You said you love me, did you mean it?"

I nodded. "I sure as fuck did."

A smile ghosted her lips. "Then focus on the fact that I said I love you, too. We'll find a way through this if it's meant to be."

I nodded even though I didn't like the *if* in that statement. But I realized she was right about one thing, we *were* meant to be. She was all high class and smart-ass, and I was scuffed boots and curse words, but somehow we worked. We smoothed out each other's edges in a way that worked. "I don't need or want an out either."

She tossed her head back and laughed. "Good, because I'm not offering you one. You're mine, pretty boy."

Damn, those words were welcome music to my ears. "That's damn good to hear, babe. Because I'm not done." She eyed me warily and took a step back and I dug into my pocket and pulled out a small red velvet bag. "I've known for a while how I felt about you, but stubborn asshole that I am, I fought it the same way I fought the reality about my leg. Until it nearly destroyed me."

Her smile was soft and sweet. "Wheeler."

"But giving in to that feeling was a hell of a lot easier and you know what else?"

"What?"

"It made me want to get better so I could enjoy being in love with you and enjoy the life we might have together. At least that's what Mitch believes."

Her brown eyes rounded and she pushed those red glasses up her nose. "You've talked to Mitch?"

I nodded. "This isn't just lip service anymore, babe." I winked and she rolled her eyes. "To prove that, I'm giving you this. As a promise." I held my breath and pulled the necklace from the bag, letting it dangle over my forefinger. "This necklace is my promise to you that I will get better. I will be better and not just for you. For us and the life we're gonna have together."

She inspected the pale gold necklace with the pink rose in soft, delicate rose gold. "It's beautiful, Wheeler."

"You're beautiful," I told her honestly. "The necklace is just like you, delicate, strong and gorgeous."

She blinked and tears fell down her cheeks. "Wheeler, dammit, you made me cry."

I smiled and pulled her close, fastening the necklace behind her. "I'll take tears of joy any day, but maybe you can learn to laugh when you're happy instead?"

Stunned, she looked up at me and laughed. The sound was welcome and loud and contagious as hell, making it easy to join in. "I'll see what I can do." Her smile dimmed and she looked me in the eyes, holding the delicate rose between her thumb and forefinger. "This is one promise I'm gonna hold you to, Wheeler."

"Damn straight you will," I told her and pulled her in for a kiss so hot and so filthy that a little old lady in thick black rimmed glasses banged on the window.

"Get a room!"

We broke apart, laughing and panting, unable to tear our eyes away from each other. "That's an excellent idea," AB said with a sultry smile. "Your place or mine?"

"Yes," I said simply and she laughed, weaving our fingers together and pulling me through the maze of the hospital until we arrive at my car.

AB turned to me with a mischievous smile. "Technically this is a room."

"Minx," I growled and hopped in the driver's seat, hoping the feeling rushing through my veins in the moment would never end.

Then I looked over at Annabelle, face flushed from smiling and laughing and kissing and being in love. She laughed again, for no reason at all, and I knew that feeling would be there.

Always.

* * * *

T H E E N D

Acknowledgements

Thank you so much for making my books a success! I appreciate all of you! Thanks to all of my beta readers, street teamers, ARC readers and Facebook fans. Y'all are THE BEST!

And a huge very special thanks to Jessie! I'm such a *hot mess, but without your keen sense of organization and skills, I'd be a burny fiery inferno of hot mess!! Thank you!

And a very special thanks to my editors (who sometimes have to work all through the night! *See HOT MESS above!) Thank you for making my words make sense.

Copyright © 2019 KB Winters and BookBoyfriends Publishing LLC

KB WINTERS

About The Author

KB Winters is a Wall Street Journal and USA Today Bestselling Author of steamy hot books about Bikers, Billionaires, Bad Boys and Badass Military Men. Just the way you like them. She has an addiction to caffeine, tattoos and hard-bodied alpha males. The men in her books are very sexy, protective and sometimes bossy, her ladies are...well...*bossier*!

Living in sunny Southern California, with her five kids and three fur babies, this embarrassingly hopeless romantic writes every chance she gets!

You can reach me at Facebook.com/kbwintersauthor and at kbwintersauthor@gmail.com

Copyright © 2019 KB Winters and BookBoyfriends Publishing LLC

Printed in Great Britain
by Amazon